Roxie's Mall Madness

Best Friends

#15

Roxie's Mall Madness

Hilda Stahl

CROSSWAY BOOKS • WHEATON, ILLINOIS
A DIVISION OF GOOD NEWS PUBLISHERS

Roxie's Mall Madness.

Copyright © 1993 by Word Spinners, Inc.

Published by Crossway Books
        a division of
        Good News Publishers
        1300 Crescent Street
        Wheaton, Illinois 60187.

Cover illustration: Paul Casale

Art Direction/Design: Mark Schramm

First printing, 1993

Printed in the United States of America

Library of Congress Cataloging-in-Publication Data
Stahl, Hilda.
    Roxie's mall madness / Hilda Stahl.
       p.   cm. — (Best Friends ; #15)
    Summary: Twelve-year-old Roxie prays for guidance in helping her sister Lacy and her brother Eli, both of whom have been acting strangely and may be in trouble.
    [1. Christian life—Fiction.   2. Brothers and sisters—Fiction.]
I. Title.   II. Series: Stahl, Hilda. Best Friends #15.
PZ7.S78244Rr 1993   [Fic]—dc20   93-22575
ISBN 0-89107-753-7

01		00		99		98		97		96		95		94		93
15	14	13	12	11	10	9	8	7	6	5	4	3	2	1

To Melissa Kutrubes
Thanks, friend

Contents

1

Families

Roxie Shoulders flipped open the *King's Kids* notebook, then dropped to her carpeted bedroom floor beside the Best Friends—Chelsea McCrea, who was president because she'd started the business of doing odd jobs for others as a way to make money; Hannah Shigwam, the treasurer because she was good with money; and Kathy Aber, the vice president because that had been the only position left. Roxie smiled. She was the secretary because her handwriting was the best. Lately she'd noticed she wrote so fast, it was hard to read what she'd written. When that happened, she'd always rewrite it as neatly as she possibly could. She didn't want to lose her position as secretary.

Frowning slightly, Chelsea looked around the circle they made. Late-afternoon sunlight shone through the two windows that flanked the nicely made bed. "Ever since Christmas we haven't had much business. Last week we helped with Heather Robbins's Valentine Day party, and tonight we're going to baby-sit ten kids at the church, but otherwise . . ."

Roxie rolled her eyes. "Chel, we know that." Roxie looked at the notes she'd already written. "Five couples are getting together at the church to plan a party for the young married couples, so they hired us to baby-sit while they meet."

Kathy nodded. "And we already know what to do since we all baby-sit often—especially with our own sisters or brothers."

"Baby-sitting right at the church nursery will make our job much easier," Hannah said. "They have toys and lots of room to play."

Roxie impatiently tapped her pencil on the notebook. "I want to talk about the assignment Marsha gave us for Sunday school—to observe the members in our family. I think it's a dumb thing to have to do, don't you?"

Hannah giggled as she flipped back her long, black hair. "It's pretty easy for me to do. Burke is learning to crawl, so I wrote that down. The twins play with their dolls when they aren't in school. Lena thinks she's really important if she can talk on the phone to Heather Robbins or whoever else will talk. Mom takes care of the family, and Dad is an engineer at a factory. What else is there for me to write?"

Looking thoughtful, Kathy pulled her jean-clad knees to her chin. Her tight, blonde curls touched the shoulders of her soft, green sweater. "I think Marsha wants us to see what motivates them to do what they do. We're supposed to find out what each person likes and dislikes and why. I already learned that my dad sometimes would rather have long hair and wear strange clothes like he did before he became lead musician for Ralph Gentry's TV show. Do you know how embarrassed I was when my dad had a ponytail?" Kathy shuddered. "And I learned my mom sometimes wishes she could stay home instead of teach school. That would be sooo strange! Mom has taught school as long as I can remember."

Chelsea twisted a long strand of red hair around her finger. "I learned my mom sometimes wishes we still lived in Oklahoma. I was really surprised because she never talks about it. Now when I see a sad look on her face, I know why she's sad."

Roxie frowned. "I know something is making Lacy cry a lot, but she won't talk to me about it. I asked her, and she told me to mind my own business. She's seventeen, so she thinks I'm a nobody because I'm only twelve."

Hannah's eyes lit up. She loved solving mysteries. "I think you should watch Lacy, listen to her, and see what you can learn. Maybe she broke up with her boyfriend, or maybe something is upsetting her at work or school. Talk to her friends. Watch her at work. I'll help if you want."

Roxie's eyes widened. "Are you kidding? Lacy would get sooo mad if she thought we were spying on her."

Sparks flew from Kathy's eyes. "I know I'd be really mad if anybody spied on me!"

"I guess none of us would like it." Chelsea pushed the sleeves of her blue and white sweater up her freckled arms. "Maybe we can find a way to help Lacy without spying on her."

Hannah glanced at the clock on Roxie's nightstand. "It's almost time to go."

Just then Roxie's dad called from the bottom of the stairs, "Roxie, girls, it's time to leave." He was taking them to the church. Kathy's dad would pick them up later.

Roxie jumped up, pushed her notebook into her desk drawer, then hurried after the girls. She enviously glanced back toward Lacy's bedroom—the master bedroom, with its own bath. Lacy got that room because Mom and Dad had their bedroom on the main floor, and she was the oldest son or daughter. Roxie hurried past Faye's room and past Eli's room. All the bedrooms were large, but Lacy's was the largest. Roxie planned to make it her room once Lacy left home for college—unless Eli decided he wanted it. It was hard to be the third child!

Several minutes later the Best Friends hung their winter jackets on the rack in the church hall outside the nursery and hurried inside. The lights were on, but the room was empty. Roxie opened the toy box and put a few toys out on the carpeted floor. Chelsea wheeled two red plastic cars from the big closet. Kathy made sure the crib had a clean sheet and blanket. Hannah set the bag of animal crackers she'd brought on a shelf. She took one out, a camel, and ate it. It crunched in her teeth and tasted sweet.

The parents came all at the same time, talking and laughing. Kathy wrote the children's names on masking tape and stuck them to their backs. There were four girls and six boys. The parents walked away, still talking and laughing. Kathy laid the youngest child, two-month-old Gabrielle, in the crib away from the toddlers. The oldest child, a four-year-old boy named Eric, ran to a car and raced around the room with a loud shout.

Roxie sat on the floor with Seth and Austin and built a wall of blocks for them to knock down. She laughed and helped them build it back up.

Hannah snapped the snaps on the back of a doll's dress for Brittany while Allie and Wesley looked on.

Chelsea caught Eric and showed him where he could ride so he wouldn't run over anyone.

When the kids were playing well by themselves, the Best Friends sat on the floor near the crib and talked about the good deed they'd do before the end of the week. They'd done a good deed once a week since they'd become Best Friends.

"We could watch the kids tonight without pay," Hannah said. "That could be our good deed."

Chelsea shook her head. "We already agreed on the pay. We'll have to think of something else. Besides, I need the money."

Giggling, Kathy leaned forward. "I know the perfect thing!"

"What?"

Kathy's eyes twinkled. "You can watch Megan for me so I can go ice-skating with Roy Marks tomorrow after school."

Hannah frowned. "I thought your dad wouldn't let you go with him."

Kathy wrinkled her nose. "I can't go with him. But I can meet him there while I'm ice-skating with a bunch of other kids."

Hannah smiled. "Me too. I'm going ice-skating with Colin Mayhew at the park Saturday."

Roxie knew Hannah had been spending a lot of time with Colin since he'd stopped living in fear of aliens taking over the world.

Chelsea suddenly jabbed Roxie. "I almost forgot the worst news I've ever heard!"

Roxie's heart sank. Was Chelsea going to say Rob liked someone else? Roxie bit her lip. She had thought Rob liked her as much as she liked him.

"Tell us!" Hannah and Kathy said together.

Chelsea took a deep breath. "Rob told me he heard this at his job yesterday." Rob worked in a store just outside The Ravines.

Roxie locked her icy hands together. It wasn't about Rob liking her or not liking her! Now she could handle hearing the news.

"A few houses in the area have been broken into in the past two weeks. The police don't know who did it. Rob said he heard a high-school boy telling another boy he thought he knew who it was. But Rob had to carry out a bag of groceries and didn't get to hear who the boy suspected."

"I have it!" Hannah's face glowed with excitement. "Our good deed is to find out who broke into the houses."

Roxie groaned as Kathy and Chelsea said, "That's impossible."

Hannah's face fell. "I guess so."

The baby cried, and Kathy jumped up to tend her. She needed her diaper changed, so Kathy changed her, fed her, and then laid her back on her stomach in the crib.

"We have to think of a good deed," Chelsea said thoughtfully as she helped dress a doll.

Just then Austin burst into tears because Wesley took a ball from him, and Roxie hurried to take care of them. "You boys can share the ball. Roll it back and forth to each other." She showed them how, then left them playing.

Later the girls gathered the kids together, sat them quietly on the floor, and gave them animal crackers to eat. There wasn't time to talk again about good deeds or boys or the news Rob had heard.

Later Roxie thought about the break-ins as she slipped on her pajamas. What if someone tried to break into *their* house? Shivers trickled down her spine. She peeked out her window at the yard below. Streetlights glowed across the street and driveways. "Heavenly Father, You said You were with us always and would keep us safe. Thank You for protecting us from guys who might try to break in. In Jesus' name, Amen."

Roxie strained her neck to try to see the McCreas' home, but she couldn't see it. Lacy could look out her window and see the McCreas' house, but she didn't have any reason to want to see it.

Sighing, Roxie turned away from her window. Should she see if Lacy would let her look out her window? "Why even try? She won't let me."

Roxie clicked off her light and stood in the middle of her room. Would she ever be able to be both Lacy's friend and sister?

Impatiently Roxie pushed the thought aside. Lacy wasn't interested in being friends.

Roxie flipped back her covers, then stopped

and listened. She heard sobs coming from Lacy's room. Why was Lacy crying? Roxie started to get into bed, then stopped. She had to try to help Lacy again.

Slowly Roxie walked to Lacy's door and knocked a tiny little knock. "Lacy, it's me."

Lacy grew quiet, then whispered, "Go back to bed, Roxie."

"I want to help you."

"You can't!"

"Please let me."

"No! I told you that before."

"But I feel so bad for you!"

"Just go to bed!"

"Please, Lacy."

"Go to bed," Lacy said tiredly.

Tears wetting her eyes, Roxie walked to her room and slowly slipped into bed. "Jesus, comfort Lacy, and give her a good night's sleep," Roxie whispered. She brushed at her eyes with her pajama sleeve, then lay there looking at her ceiling.

2

A Good Deed

Roxie walked off the school bus right behind Stacia King, the African-American girl who lived with her grandparents at The Ravines so she could go to Middle Lake Middle School. Stacia's long, frizzy hair, held back with a wide, red ribbon, hung down over her red jacket. She wanted to be a famous singer someday. Shouts from the other kids getting off the bus filled the air. Kids threw snowballs back and forth. A new snow perfect for snowballs and snowmen had fallen during the afternoon. Everyone was glad it was Friday. Roxie was glad because she was going to have a sleepover with the Best Friends at Chelsea's. They tried to have a sleepover every Friday night.

Stacia waited and fell into step with Roxie. Stacia lived on Hannah's side of the street several houses down. "Did you read the announcement about the Spring Cantata?"

Roxie nodded. "I was in it last year. I guess I'll sign up for it again. Will you?" Stacia was the best singer her age Roxie had ever heard.

Stacia smiled and nodded. "I sing every chance I can get."

"Yeah, me too." Roxie giggled. "Not really. I don't sing very well, but I like to sing anyway." Just then she spotted a snowman standing in a yard. She stopped to look at it, and Stacia stopped beside her. "Don't you love it?" The snowman was about six feet tall with a top hat and cane—a magnificent Frosty the Snowman.

"I like to see snowmen in the yards. Where I lived before, the snow got dirty too fast to build a snowman, and there really wasn't enough room to build one anyway."

"Eli likes building snowmen." Roxie smiled as she remembered the different ones he'd made down through the years. Sometimes he even let her help him. "One year he made a snow bench and had a snowman sitting on it like he was waiting for a bus or something. It was great."

"Grandma says the woman next door, Priscilla Adgate, always has the best snowman in the neighborhood, but this year she's sick and can't build one."

Roxie's eyes widened. "We've been trying to think of a good deed to do. That's what it'll be! . . . building a snowman for Mrs. Adgate! I know right where she lives. We helped with her yard work last fall."

"I'll help if you want me to, but I'm not that good in the cold."

"Chelsea, Hannah, and Kathy will be helping me, but you're welcome to join in. Or you can just watch if it makes you too cold to help." Roxie was so excited about the thought of building a snowman for Mrs. Adgate, she could barely stand still. "As soon as I get home I'll call her and get permission to build a snowman for her."

"Why can't you just surprise her?"

"With the scare of the break-ins she might think we're there to make trouble and call the police or something. Besides, we can't trespass even to do a good deed."

"I guess you're right."

Roxie hurried along with Stacia and stopped once to see a snowman in another yard. "I like seeing flowers in the summer and snowmen in the winter. Wouldn't it be strange to live in a place where it doesn't snow?"

Stacia shivered. "Sometimes I wish I did! I hate being cold!"

"Maybe when you become a famous recording star you can live in the South."

"Maybe." Stacia didn't sound very sure. "I've heard it's still hard in the South to live next door to whites like we can here at The Ravines."

Roxie flushed as they started walking again. Sometimes it was hard for her not to be prejudiced.

"My grandma said a few years ago in the South they had public drinking fountains for whites and another one for blacks. Blacks had to ride in the back of the bus too, never in the front. I wouldn't want to live like that."

"That would be terrible. I saw a TV show about a black woman who dared to drink from the water fountain for whites. She was actually beat up because of what she did!" Roxie shivered. She was never that prejudiced!

Just then they reached Roxie's house. "I'll see you later maybe."

Stacia nodded. "Have fun building the snowman."

"We will." Smiling, Roxie ran into her house. Warm air wrapped around her as she slipped off her jacket. The smell of varnish floated up the basement steps and blended with the aroma of coffee from the kitchen. "I'm home," she called.

"In the kitchen," Mom called back.

Roxie hurried to the kitchen where Mom and Faye sat at the table coloring in Faye's coloring book. There was something different about Mom. Then Roxie realized Mom no longer had streaks of gray hair. "Mom! Your hair!"

Mom laughed self-consciously as she fluffed her shoulder-length, light brown hair. "Do you like it?"

21

"I do! Has Dad seen it?"

"Not yet. But I think he'll like it too."

Roxie laughed. Sometimes Dad had a hard time accepting change, and he was the first to admit it.

Faye moved until her head touched Mom's. "See? Our hair is the same color. Now we're twins!"

"Except you're about thirty-five years younger than Mom," Roxie said with a laugh as she pulled the phone book out of the drawer.

Frowning, Faye looked at Mom. "Is that true?"

Laughing, Mom kissed Faye's cheek. "It's true. I couldn't be your age and be your mother, you know. And I like being your mother."

Roxie found Priscilla Adgate's phone number and held her finger on it. "What made you decide to color your hair now?"

Mom shrugged. "Gray hair made me look older than I am. Just yesterday somebody thought I was Faye's grandmother!"

"That's terrible! I'm glad you colored it." Roxie ran her fingers through her dark hair. "I wish I had light brown hair like yours instead of dark brown!"

"But yours is so pretty!" Mom smiled. "In fact, I almost colored mine the same as yours, but I decided to stay as close to the natural color as possible."

"I will never get gray hair," Faye said firmly as she went back to her coloring.

"Not as long as there is color in a bottle," Mom said with a laugh.

As Roxie picked up the phone to call Mrs. Adgate, she explained to Mom why she was calling. "How nice," Mom said.

Mrs. Adgate answered on the third ring. Roxie told her what she wanted to do. "We want to do this just for the fun of it. So, is it all right if we come over tonight to build a snowman for you?"

"How precious! Of course it's all right." Mrs. Adgate sounded close to tears. "I was looking out the window just this afternoon wishing for a snow-man. I'll see you later."

Smiling, Roxie said good-bye and hung up. "I think I might make a dog snow-sculpture for her too. That would be fun to do."

Faye jumped off her chair and ran over to Roxie. "Make a little girl snowman like me!" Faye twirled around, sending her skirt swirling away from her legs and her long ponytail flipping around excitedly. Faye liked dressing in dresses more than in jeans.

"I'll think about it," Roxie said.

Later when Roxie met with the Best Friends at Chelsea's house, she told them her idea. "And Faye wants us to make a little snowgirl."

Chelsea's eyes sparkled. "Let's do it!"

"We'll make a family," Hannah said excitedly.

"This'll be a fun good deed." Kathy laughed as

she moved her sleeping bag against the basement wall. "Let's go before it gets too dark to work."

A few minutes later the Best Friends stopped in the Adgates' front yard. Flower beds were covered with snow. Tall winter-bare trees lined the sidewalk. Snow blanketed the evergreen bushes that stood along the front of the house.

Setting down the bag of hats, scarfs, and other stuff to use on the snowmen, Roxie looked next door to where Stacia lived. All the houses in The Ravines were built alike, but were painted different colors. Stacia's house was white with blue shutters. The Adgates' house was cream-colored with a brown roof and brown shutters. "Stacia said she might come help us—if she doesn't feel too cold."

"Good. Let's start. We'll make the snowman family up near the evergreen bushes where they'll show off the best." Laughing excitedly, Chelsea started rolling a snowball across the yard. It got bigger and bigger as she rolled it, leaving behind a line of bare grass.

Kathy and Hannah started rolling snowballs across the yard, while Roxie figured out the best way to make the dog. This was different from just an ordinary snowman. She decided she'd make a Dalmatian sitting on its haunches with a long tail and pointed ears that flopped over.

Laughing because of the fun she was going to have, Roxie started her own snowball. Music drifted out from the house across the street. In the distance a siren wailed. This was going to be the best-looking yard in the entire subdivision!

A couple of little boys carrying sleds stopped to watch, then ran off toward the park.

■

Brushing away tears, Priscilla Adgate looked out her window. It was nice of the girls to make a snowman for her front yard. She'd almost refused to let the girls come, but she had wanted a snowman so badly, she couldn't turn them down. She bit back a sigh. How she'd like to help them! But they thought she was sick. She'd told Mrs. Smith next door she wasn't feeling well, but she hadn't told her the truth. Actually she was too depressed to do anything except go to work because she had to to keep up the house payments. She should've gone with Gene on his business trip, but she couldn't even do that.

Priscilla pulled the curtain wider and waved to the girls. They waved happily back. "To be young again!" she said with a catch in her voice. She felt more like fifty instead of thirty-eight. If she could go back in time, she wouldn't make the same mistakes. Maybe then her son Tad would love her. She frowned and dropped the curtain. She dare not start thinking about Tad or she'd start to cry again and never stop. She looked at his picture when he was eleven on the fireplace mantel, then quickly away.

■

Outdoors Roxie stepped back and studied the beginnings of the Dalmatian. She could see the haunches, but the rest just looked like a short, thin snowman. Could she really carve a dog out of the mound of snow? She'd carved one out of wood with her tools, but now she was using her hands.

Her cheeks bright red, Chelsea patted her snowman. It was taller than she was and had a carrot nose, black walnuts for eyes, and a twig for a smiling mouth. It was the father of the family. "It needs eyebrows."

"Use a piece off the evergreen bush." Hannah pointed to the eyebrows on her snowman. It was the mother of the family. "Make sure you don't make your snowman look like a woman."

Kathy put a red knit cap on her snowman. It was the child of the family.

Just then Roxie looked at the front window. She frowned. "Mrs. Adgate can't see the faces!"

Chelsea tipped her head thoughtfully, then giggled. "Let's put faces on the backs too! That way you can enjoy the front or the back."

"Great idea." Roxie nodded as she set to work again on the dog. "I'll put the dog sideways so Mrs. Adgate can enjoy it more." Roxie carefully reworked part of the base until the dog was looking across the yard instead of out to the street. It was perfect.

Roxie's hands tingled with cold through her soggy mittens, but she ignored them. She wanted to finish the dog before dark. The streetlights didn't shed enough light to work by.

Finally the snow scene was finished, and the girls stood back and looked in pride at it. They were chilled to the bone, and their jeans were soaked, but they didn't care. They'd finished their good deed. They held hands and bowed their heads. They always prayed for the ones they did the good deed for.

"Father in Heaven, take care of Mrs. Adgate and her family," Chelsea prayed in her Oklahoma accent. "Bless them and meet all of their needs. If there is anything we can do to help them, let us know and help us to do it. In Jesus' name, Amen."

"Amen," the others echoed.

Roxie ran to the door and rang the bell. She pulled a card from her pocket they'd signed for Mrs. Adgate.

Priscilla opened the door a crack. She didn't want them to see her red-rimmed eyes and puffy eyelids. "I can't invite you in," she said.

"That's all right. I have something for you." Roxie pushed the card through the crack.

"Thank you." Priscilla held it close to her.

"Look out the window and see what you think," Roxie said just as Priscilla was closing the door.

Priscilla hurried to the living room and pulled back the curtain. She gasped in delight. Before she knew she was going to, she laughed right out loud. It had been weeks since she'd laughed like that. She waved to the girls.

They laughed and waved back, then turned to walk away.

Priscilla looked at the snow family and the dog for a long time. Finally she opened the card. It said, "Get well soon. We're praying for you. John 3:16. Chelsea, Roxie, Hannah, and Kathy."

Priscilla held the card to her heart. She couldn't remember having anyone pray for her since she'd stopped going to Sunday school when she was a teenager. She did remember the Bible verse mentioned in the card, and she recited it aloud, then burst into fresh tears.

■

Outdoors the girls stopped at Stacia's house and rang the bell. Stacia opened the door.

"Want to come look?" Roxie asked.

Stacia nodded. "Let me get my jacket." She grabbed it out of the closet and hurried next door with the girls. "I'm sorry I couldn't help. Grandma and I were playing Scrabble."

Roxie flung out her hand. "Ta daaa!"

Stacia gasped in delight. "I've never seen anything like it! I've got to get Grandma and Grandpa and show them."

"We have to get home before we freeze," Chelsea said. "See you, Stacia."

"Bye." Stacia ran to her house and hurried inside.

The Best Friends smiled at each other, then ran to Chelsea's house. Their good deed was done. It wasn't much, but it had pleased Mrs. Adgate.

Roxie peeled off her wet mittens and jacket. She was shivering so hard, it was almost impossible to pull off her boots. She smiled, feeling good deep down in her heart. She'd never done good deeds before she met the Best Friends. Now that she knew how wonderful it felt, she was going to help others for the rest of her life.

"How about some hot chocolate?" Chelsea asked.

"Yes!" Roxie shouted, already feeling the warmth it would bring and already tasting the sweet chocolate.

3

The Sleepover

Roxie sat at the counter in Chelsea's basement and sipped the hot chocolate. She felt snug and warm and happy. She'd changed into dry jeans, a soft pink sweater, and warm pink socks. They almost always had their sleepovers at Chelsea's because her whole basement was a fabulous rec room with a big-screen TV, a pool table, a Ping-Pong table, and a kitchenette. They would bring their sleeping bags and sleep on the carpeted floor. Roxie set her cup down and wiped a melted marshmallow mustache off her upper lip. She laid the white paper napkin beside her cup and turned to Chelsea. "Did you see Kesha in gym today?" Kesha was the girl who'd convinced Chelsea to change her look to get attention when she'd first started school at Middle Lake Middle School. It had caused a lot of trouble for Chelsea, but in the end she'd learned to be herself. And Kesha had become a real friend.

Nodding, Chelsea set down her cup of cocoa. "She is really getting good on the mat. She's thinking about becoming a gymnast. Mike watched her one day, and he thinks she's good too." Mike was Chelsea's eight-year-old brother who was planning to go to the Olympics someday as a gymnast.

"She sure is different now that she's living with Mrs. Murphy." Kathy reached for a cookie. Kesha's dad couldn't quite manage to take care of his family, so Mrs. Murphy had taken Kesha as her foster daughter. They had learned to love each other immediately and helped each other with everything.

Chelsea gasped. "I just remembered that Mrs. Murphy wants us to come over sometime next week. She has a job for us. I don't know what it is. She called me yesterday, and I forgot to mention it."

Roxie wasn't sure how that would fit in with her schedule. She had planned to observe her other family members some more after getting home on Monday, for the Sunday school assignment.

Her red brows cocked, Chelsea glanced at the others. "Are you all free?"

Kathy and Hannah nodded.

"I'm not sure which day would work best for me," Roxie said as she picked up her cup. She liked the way the melted marshmallow covered the top of the cocoa. "You girls can go without me if you need to."

Chelsea grabbed a notepad and jotted down

the information. "Okay. We'll see what works best."

Hannah washed her empty cup and set it on the counter so it would drain. They always had to clean up after themselves when they had a sleepover. None of them minded doing that. They were all used to helping at home. Hannah turned away from the sink. "Today I heard Pamela Woods talking about the things she has to do at home." Hannah sat on a tall stool at the snack bar. "She was really mad because her mom makes her make her bed every morning and unload the dishwasher after dinner at night. Can you believe she thinks she has to work too hard?"

Kathy groaned. "She doesn't have a little sister or a mom who has a career or she'd have to do a whole lot more. I know!"

Hannah rolled her eyes. "I don't know how it would feel if that little bit was all I ever had to do!"

Roxie leaned her elbows on the tall counter. "You can't believe how much I have to do now that Lacy's working at the department store. Before she had this job, we shared the work. Dad said the only reason they had kids was to help around the house—cheap labor, he said." Roxie giggled. "He was only kidding, of course."

"I need to ask you girls something." Hannah pushed back her hair and looked very serious.

"What?" they asked together.

"What do you think of Colin Mayhew?"

The girls groaned. Roxie jabbed Hannah. "We already know you like him. We all think he's a nice guy."

"You can talk about him if you want." Chelsea giggled. "And I'll talk about Brody." Brody was Kathy's foster brother, and Chelsea had liked him for several weeks. They'd even exchanged valentines.

"Doesn't it bother you that Colin has . . . you know . . . a big nose?" Hannah flushed painfully.

"Maybe he'll grow into it," Kathy said.

"His dad didn't." Hannah pushed her hands into her pockets and walked away from the counter. "You should see his nose! It's huge!"

"You can't like or not like someone because of his looks." Roxie scowled. "Lacy does, but it's not fair. I decided I'd never be that way."

Frowning, Kathy leaned against the counter. "I'd sure hate to like an ugly boy. Everybody would laugh."

"So what?" Chelsea flipped back her flame-red hair. "Have you ever noticed that after you get to know somebody who's not good-looking you don't even notice their looks?"

"It's the same even if they're really good-looking. Pretty soon you don't even notice. You see them for who they are." Roxie spread her hands wide. "It's really strange, isn't it?"

HILDA STAHL

"I'm tired of talking about boys." Chelsea ran to the table where Clue was set out to play. "I'm ready for a game. Anyone else?"

They all ran to the table and were soon engrossed in the competition. Hannah was usually the best at the game. Today she won two games, and Kathy won one. After that they flopped down on giant pillows and watched a movie on the VCR. It was a romantic comedy that made the girls laugh and cry.

■

At Priscilla Adgate's house she tied her robe around her slender waist, then held to her heart the note that Roxie had given her. "They're praying for me," she whispered over and over. "God does love me. He does know my heart is broken. He wants to help me."

She peeked out the window at the snow family and the dog. Would she ever be able to tell the girls what a blessing they were to her? Why would the girls even think to do this for her? It had to be God showing her He loved her.

The phone rang, and she jumped, then hurried to answer it. She sank to the blue armchair and curled her feet under her.

"Priscilla, it's Gene. How are you, hon?"

"Fine," she managed to say. "I miss you a lot."

"I wish you were with me. Anything interesting happen today?"

34

She told him about the girls building the snow family and the dog. "I hope they're still here when you get back next week."

"I heard the weather report. It's supposed to stay cold there."

"What's new with you?"

Gene sighed. "I've been able to present my report to a couple of men, but I don't know how it'll match up against the competition."

"You did a lot of background checking. It has to be competitive."

"I guess."

"Is it warm there?"

"Yes. No snow at all, of course. You'd like it."

"I guess, but I like the snow too."

Gene was quiet a while. "Did your son call you?"

Priscilla stiffened. "Tad won't have anything to do with me. You know that."

"I know that when he grows up a little he'll see that you aren't the monster your ex-husband says you are."

"I wish." She struggled to hold back the tears.

"Get a good night's sleep, hon. I'll call you tomorrow night."

"I love you, Gene." Priscilla hung up and leaned back in the chair. This wasn't a good time to be alone, but she couldn't keep Gene home just because of her terrible depression.

The phone rang again, and she jumped. Gene must've forgotten to tell her something. She picked up the receiver. "Hi."

"Mom?"

She stiffened. "Tad!"

"Don't get any ideas, Mom. I'm not calling to say I changed my mind and want to live with you. I need some money. Can you help me out?"

She bit her lip. She'd promised herself she wouldn't give him any more money after the last time. But she couldn't refuse over the phone, or she might never see him again. "Stop in tomorrow, and we'll talk about it."

"Talk? I don't need to talk. I need the money. How much can you give me?"

"What about your dad? He has custody of you."

"He won't give me any more. He says I should get a job."

Priscilla's throat almost closed with tears. How she longed to have her son with her! She wanted to hold him close and never let him go. "Tad, you'd like working at a job. Not just for the money, but because it would make you feel good to make an income for yourself."

"Does that mean no, Mom?" he snapped.

She bent over in agony as she gripped the phone. She knew she had to refuse for Tad's sake, but it was so hard! "Why do you need the money?"

"Does it matter?"

"If you need clothes, we could go shopping tomorrow. I could buy you clothes."

"You'll be sorry you didn't give me money when I needed it!"

"Tad, I love you."

"Sure . . . I bet." He slammed down the phone.

The loud *click* hurt her ear. With a sob from deep inside she hung up the receiver. She covered her face with both hands and cried deep sobs that tore through her, leaving her weak.

At Chelsea's the girls stretched out on their sleeping bags with a nightlight glowing in the kitchenette. Music from the tape player played softly. They weren't allowed to have it so loud it would disturb the others in the house.

Suddenly Roxie sat up. "Let's pray for Priscilla Adgate again." Roxie flushed. Why had she thought of Mrs. Adgate? Roxie shrugged. What did it matter? She had thought of her, so she knew they needed to pray for her.

The girls gathered in a circle, held hands, and prayed for Priscilla Adgate.

At Priscilla's house a peace settled over her that she couldn't understand. She slowly walked to her bedroom and slipped into bed. She fell asleep immediately, something she hadn't done in a long time.

37

∎

The Best Friends looked at each other, smiled, and slipped back into their sleeping bags. Roxie smiled. She might never know why she'd suddenly felt such an urgency to pray for Mrs. Adgate, but she was glad that they had.

"Thank You, Jesus," Roxie said under her breath. Aloud she said, "Isn't prayer funny? You talk to someone you don't see, and you expect an answer."

The girls laughed. Chelsea lifted up the top part of her body and rested her head on her hand, with her elbow resting on the floor. She was wearing her favorite Oklahoma nightshirt. "When I was little, I thought God was like my grandpa—ready to listen and help. Then I found out Grandpa couldn't take care of *everything* because he could only be in one place at a time. I asked him how God could take care of everyone all over. Grandpa said God was everywhere and could see everyone at the same time, and yet God knew all the details about each person. Of course, I couldn't understand how that could be, but I liked thinking about it, and I knew it was true even if I didn't understand it. When we pray for someone who's somewhere else, God really can take care of them. Like when we prayed for Mrs. Adgate—God gave her peace because we asked Him to."

Hannah flopped on her stomach and rested her

chin in her hands. "I heard about a missionary, Susan Eldry, who was in danger of being killed. But nobody knew it. One night Ellen Morgan, a woman my mom knows, woke up from a sound sleep and 'saw' the missionary as if she were standing right there in the bedroom. Ellen Morgan knew God was asking her to pray for the missionary's safety, so she did. A year later the missionary, Susan Eldry, was speaking in the church Ellen attended. Susan told about a miraculous escape she'd made when someone was going to kill her. She told the exact time and date. Ellen said chills ran down her spine because it was right when she'd been awakened to pray for Susan Eldry. Distance doesn't matter to God because He's everywhere."

Kathy sat up and wrapped her arms around her drawn-up legs. "Dad told us Ralph Gentry gets letters from people all over who watch his TV show. They tell about God answering prayer for them when Ralph Gentry prayed for them. When I try to imagine how it happens, I can't. I just know God does answer prayer for others even if they live a long way away from the person who's praying."

"Because distance is nothing to God," Roxie said softly. "He's everywhere all the time. Dad read a Scripture to us—I don't remember where it is in the Bible, but it said God searches all over the earth for someone to bless. He's looking at us right now to bless us." Roxie pressed her hand to her heart as the reality of God seeing her and wanting to bless her sunk in. She smiled. "Isn't that awesome!"

"Awesome," the Best Friends whispered.

Smiling, Roxie closed her eyes and drifted into peaceful sleep.

4

Eli

Ready to burst with excitement, Roxie ran upstairs to tell Eli the great news that one of her carvings Grandma had taken to the craft show in Detroit had been sold. Grandma had called from a pay phone, too excited to wait until they got home. Roxie laughed under her breath. She was sooo glad she and Eli were friends as well as brother and sister. He'd be as excited about the sale as she was.

She reached his bedroom, but when she heard the sound of voices coming through the half-open door she stopped short in the hallway. She hadn't known he had company. She'd tell him later. Sighing, she started to walk away, then stopped when she heard what Eli was saying. Her heart lodged in her throat, then plunged all the way to her feet.

"Don't make me steal a copy of the exam, Nate!"

Nate! Eli couldn't possibly be talking with Nate Irwin, the African-American boy who'd been arrested last month for robbing a convenience store!

"It's the only way, Shoulders."

Roxie shook her head and nervously rubbed her hands up and down her arms. It couldn't be *that* Nate. Eli would never associate with him. She started to walk away, but Nate's words stopped her.

"We need another man, Shoulders. You'd be perfect because nobody would suspect a Christian guy like you." Nate chuckled. "It'll send a thrill through you like nothing you've done before. Trust me."

Roxie's mouth turned dust-dry. Eli wouldn't really steal a copy of an exam, would he?

"You're right about that," Eli said. "All right, Nate. I could use the money."

"Meet me later tonight at the mall near The Jeans Outlet."

"It'll be hard. I'm not supposed to stay out late."

Roxie's stomach knotted painfully. She crept to her room and sank to the edge of her bed. Outside her windows that flanked her bed, snow swirled in the overcast sky. Her head spun with what to do about Eli. Mom and Dad had taken Faye to get shoes at the mall, and Lacy was at work. Roxie bit her lip. How could she help Eli? He was too easily persuaded! Dad had talked to him about that lots of times. She could not let Eli get in trouble with Nate Irwin!

Roxie jumped up, then stopped with her hands on the waist of her jeans. Would Eli get mad at her for bursting in on him while Nate was there? Heat rushed over her and turned her face and neck red. No matter what, she'd stop Eli!

She ran down the carpeted hall to Eli's room. The door was wide open, and the room was empty! His bed was neatly made. Books and a computer sat on his desk. She ran downstairs and reached the front door just as Eli was closing it.

He turned with a laugh, his eyes twinkling behind his glasses. "What's the rush?"

She caught his arm. His green sweater felt soft and warm to her touch. His hair was as dark as hers and cut short. "I heard you talking to Nate! Please *please* don't do it!"

Eli jabbed his glasses against his face and frowned. "How dare you eavesdrop outside my door?"

She swallowed hard. How she hated for him to yell at her! "I didn't mean to."

"Don't do it again!" He pulled away from her. "It's my business what I do, so stay out of it!"

Tears filled her eyes. "Why are you acting this way? I only want to help you!"

"You're butting in where you're not wanted!" Eli brushed past her and hurried to the kitchen.

43

Roxie dashed to the kitchen after him. She wouldn't let him do this! She found him sticking his head into the refrigerator searching for something to eat. He pulled out a small bowl of leftover mashed potatoes and stuck them in the microwave.

Stopping at the island counter, Roxie nervously pushed back her short, dark hair. "Can we at least talk about it, Eli?"

"No." He kept his back to her. His sweater hung loosely over his jeans.

Roxie cleared her tight throat. "You know the trouble Nate's been in."

"So?"

Roxie's temper flared, and she grabbed Eli's arm. "You know what trouble *you* could be in if you start hanging out with him!"

"Leave me alone, Roxann Shoulders! I don't know why I ever thought we could get along."

Her face ashen, Roxie fell back. She'd worked so hard to make friends with Eli! How could he just toss her aside? For a long time they'd ignored each other or fought with each other. During the summer she'd decided to try to get to know him like she'd get to know a stranger. Little by little they'd become friends. Now he was back to yelling at her.

He gripped her arms and looked down into her face. His blue eyes flashed behind his glasses. "I want you to promise you won't say anything to

44

Mom and Dad about what you heard or about Nate being here."

His grip hurt her arms, but she didn't say so. "How come?"

"Because they'll jump to the same conclusions as you, and I don't want to be bothered. So promise!"

Her head whirled. "Oh, all right!"

"You'd better not break your word!"

"I won't. I don't ever, do I?"

"I guess not." The microwave buzzed, and Eli took out the heated potatoes. He frowned at Roxie. "Don't just stand there and watch me eat! Don't you have anything better to do?"

His words struck a harder blow than if he'd punched her. She frowned at him, then ran to the hall. She had to talk to somebody! "The Best Friends," she muttered. She'd left them this morning after the sleepover. She reached for the phone, then dropped her hand as she remembered each of them was busy on this Saturday afternoon. Hannah Shigwam was ice-skating with Colin Mayhew. Since last week when he'd stopped believing in aliens taking over the world and accepted Jesus as his Savior, he and Hannah had been doing a lot of things together. Chelsea McCrea and her family were watching her little brother Mike at a gymnastics meet in Grand Rapids. And Kathy Aber was visiting her grandma.

Roxie pushed her hands into the pockets of her jeans and looked wildly around. This was like before she'd had friends, before Chelsea had come from Oklahoma and moved in next door. Slowly they'd become friends, along with Hannah Shigwam across the street and Kathy Aber who lived a short ways outside The Ravines.

Roxie wrapped her arms around herself and struggled to hold back tears. She could go to the park where Hannah and Colin were ice-skating. Roxie shook her head. She couldn't bother Hannah when she was having fun.

What could she do? Certainly she did not want to stay home in an empty house! "I'll go to the mall," she said with determination. Mom and Dad wouldn't care as long as she left a note and came home in time for dinner.

Several minutes later Roxie pushed through the doors of the mall. It was good to be inside where it was warm and crowded, with plenty of people around to take her mind off Eli. Maybe she'd see someone she knew so she wouldn't have to be alone.

She touched her pocket where she'd stuck all the money she had—ten dollars. What should she buy? She had the rest of the afternoon, so she knew she could find *something* she wanted.

Slowly she walked through the noisy crowd from store to store, her jacket over her arm. At first all she thought about was Eli, but then she started thinking about finding something to spend her money on. She went to the clearance rack at five stores, trying on skirts and blouses and sweaters. It was the middle of February, but already spring clothes were out, and winter ones were marked down. In just about every store she entered she saw Julie Pierson, a blonde-haired girl in sixth grade with her at Middle Lake Middle School. Julie never hung out with anyone at school, and she was alone today in the mall. She usually got good grades and always stayed out of trouble. In the fifth store Roxie finally said, "Hi, Julie."

"Hi, Roxie." Julie didn't smile as she shifted her jacket from one arm to the other. "What are you trying to find?"

"Nothing, actually. I'm just looking, and if I find something I want I'll get it. How about you?"

Julie shrugged, then pulled her red and black sweater down over her jeans. "I'm only looking. It's something to do."

"Yeah."

"You're usually with Chelsea, Hannah, and Kathy. How come you're alone today?"

"They're busy. Why are you alone?"

"I always am." Julie looked across the crowded store. "I guess I'll be going."

"Can I go with you?"

"Sure."

Roxie walked out of the store with Julie and

onto the crowded walkway. Smells of cookies from the corner cookie store filled the area. "Did you try Gantos?"

Julie nodded. "I was in there this morning."

"I saw really great hair bands in Beverly's. Want to go there again? I think I'll buy one."

"Sure. Why not?"

In Beverly's Roxie bought two hair bands and a bow. She held a green one up to Julie's blonde hair. "This would look good on you."

"I might as well buy it." Julie laughed as she walked over to the clerk.

Later they each ate a slice of pizza and drank a can of pop. They talked about school and boys and basketball games they'd been to. Julie was fun to talk to. About an hour later Roxie dropped her paper plate, cup, and napkin in the trash container. "I guess I better go. What about you?"

"I don't know." Julie looked at her watch. "Maybe in another hour."

"See you in school Monday."

"Sure."

Roxie started to walk away. She hated to leave Julie all alone. It was no fun being alone. She looked over her shoulder and smiled.

Julie hurried after her. "I'll walk you to the doors."

Roxie smiled. "Thanks." They walked slowly down the wide corridor. "Do you live nearby?"

"On Conway. You?"

"In The Ravines."

"Oh, yeah. I've been past there a few times."

Roxie studied Julie thoughtfully. "You sure you'll be all right alone?"

Julie shrugged. "I guess."

"Okay." Roxie said good-bye, walked outdoors, and glanced up at the winter-gray sky. The cold wind flipped her hair and turned her cheeks pink. She unlocked her bike and quickly rode home. The station wagon was parked in the garage beside Dad's pickup. Roxie thought about Eli and trembled. Why had she promised Eli she wouldn't tell Mom and Dad that Nate Irwin had been there?

Roxie left her bike in the garage, then looked across the street at the igloo they'd all built last month. It had melted a little, but still stood in the Griggs family's yard next to the Shigwam house. Maybe she should run down the street to see how the snow family at the Adgates had made it through the night. It was too cold for them to have melted. She shook her head. She'd sit in the igloo a while, then go home.

Roxie ran across the street to the igloo. She dropped to all fours and called into the tunnel that led into the snow house, "Anybody in there?"

"I am."

"Hannah! I thought you were with Colin."

Roxie happily crawled inside and sat with Hannah on the green indoor/outdoor carpet.

Hannah smiled dreamily as she hugged her knees. Her long, black hair hung over her red jacket. "I wanted to be by myself to think about Colin and the fun we had."

"Want me to leave?"

"No! Of course not! I need to talk about Colin to somebody!"

Roxie thought about telling Hannah about Eli, but Hannah was so excited about Colin that she couldn't get in a word.

"He and his mom and dad are going to our church tomorrow. Isn't that great?"

"Yeah!"

"I said I'd save him a seat in Sunday school."

"Okay." Roxie sighed. It would feel funny to have Colin sitting with the Best Friends.

Finally Hannah stopped talking about Colin and asked, "Did you decide what you're going to write a report on for English?"

"No. Have you?"

"Maybe something about my Ottawa Indian culture."

"That'll be interesting. I don't know what I want to write about. It seems so dumb! Maybe I won't even do it. Who cares if I get a failing grade?"

Hannah raised her dark brows. "You care, Roxie."

Roxie rolled her eyes. "I know. It just doesn't seem important. And it's sooo boring!"

"It's not boring if you find something you really care about."

"Like what?"

"I don't know! Your family maybe."

"Sure. Like anybody would want to hear about my family."

"You've got a great family!"

Roxie thought about Eli. What would happen if Eli made a bad name for himself? How would she feel then?

"What's wrong?"

"Nothing." She couldn't tell Hannah her suspicions about Eli. For a while Hannah had loved Eli, but he had broken her heart. She'd forgiven him because Jesus said to, but she might think Eli was really terrible if she knew about his hanging around with Nate Irwin. Roxie dropped to all fours. "I gotta get home. See you tomorrow."

"I guess I'd better go home too."

Roxie crawled out of the igloo and dashed across the street without saying another word to Hannah.

5

Secrets

Roxie hung her jacket in the closet and left her sneakers on the mat. The smell of hotdogs drifted out to her, but that didn't entice her after the pizza at the mall. Actually, after her talk with Eli she'd thought she'd never eat again. But of course she'd been able to at the mall when Eli was out of her mind. Right then the only important thing was how she could spend her money.

"Is that you, Roxie?" Mom called from the kitchen.

"Yes, Mom." Roxie wanted to go to her room and not face Mom and Dad.

"Come in here, Roxie!" Dad sounded excited.

Sighing, Roxie pushed up her sweater sleeves as she walked to the kitchen. Mom and Dad, both dressed in jeans, stood at the island counter putting together hotdogs with all the trimmings. The aroma of the finely chopped onions rose from the small, white pile on the cutting board. "Hi," Roxie said in a small voice.

"Congratulations on your sale!" Mom set her hotdog on a paper plate, then rushed over to Roxie, hugged and kissed her, then held her away with a proud smile. Mom smelled like an onion. "Grandma called a few a minutes ago to see what we thought of your wonderful news. We said we hadn't heard, so she told us. She and Ezra were very excited. Grandma sold several of my pieces too, but she said selling your little wooden mouse pleased her the most."

Dad chuckled as he hugged Roxie. He smelled like mustard. He had the same dark hair and blue eyes as Roxie and Eli. "You can see your mom is excited. That's why she's talking so fast that nobody can understand her."

Roxie managed to smile but couldn't feel excited. Roxie and her mom were both good at carving things from wood. Grandma liked taking the art pieces to sell when Mom couldn't do it herself. Before Grandpa had died, he'd gone to art shows regularly with his famous carvings. Grandma always went with him. Now she was married to Ezra Menski, and they went together to art shows. Ezra couldn't do any kind of art, even though he loved to look at sculptures and paintings. It had taken Roxie several months to accept him as her new grandpa. Now she could even pet his dog

Gracie without getting angry that Grandma had dared to marry Ezra.

Mom carried her hotdog to the table and sat down. "I was over twenty when I sold my first carving. Here you are only twelve! You could be famous by the time you're twenty!"

Roxie shrugged. She liked carving—even better since she'd inherited Grandpa's special tools. But she didn't know if she wanted to devote her life to art like Grandpa had.

Dad swallowed a bite of hotdog, then chuckled. "I'm a building contractor, and you two are wood carvers. All in the family, I guess." He winked at Roxie and took another bite.

Roxie forced a laugh. Dad liked his jokes. He thought building houses was a real work of art—only a different kind of art from carving.

She leaned against the counter as Mom and Dad ate and talked to her. Finally she said, "Dad, you didn't say how you like Mom's hair."

Dad frowned as he studied Mom. "Is it different?"

Mom laughed and threw a wadded-up napkin at him. She turned to Roxie. "He likes it."

"Your mom is pretty with or without gray hair."

Roxie nodded. She had to get out of there before she told on Eli. "Where's Faye?"

Mom swallowed a bite. "In her room. She was

anxious to play with a new doll Grandma bought her recently."

"I guess I'll see what she's up to." Roxie slowly walked away. She really didn't want to see Faye, but she couldn't stay with Mom and Dad another moment or she might say something about Eli.

Roxie ran upstairs to Faye's room. For a long time Faye had been too afraid to sleep in a bedroom of her own, but now she did. Going to preschool had given her confidence to do things she'd never done before.

Roxie peeked into Faye's room, then bit back a gasp. Faye was sitting on the floor with a golden brown puppy on her lap. The puppy looked like a fat ball of fur with a pink tongue and round, black eyes. It was the most adorable puppy Roxie had ever seen. "Faye! How cute!"

Faye gasped and jerked a doll blanket over the puppy. "You didn't knock before you entered!" Faye always talked older than her years. She could already read too and was proud of it.

Roxie pulled the blanket off the puppy. "He's precious! Where'd you get him?" Roxie lifted the puppy to her face and rubbed her cheek against his thick hair.

Her blue eyes wide, Faye ran to the door and closed it. Her hair hung in two long ponytails over each ear. Pink ribbons around the tails matched her pink sweater. "Are you gonna tell on me?"

Roxie gasped. "Don't Mom and Dad know?"

Faye shook her head hard, sending her tails dancing. "I found him and brought him inside."

"Then he must belong to somebody."

"He doesn't have a collar." Faye took the puppy and held him close to her. "See? No collar. He belongs to me! I prayed for a puppy, and there he was waiting right in our backyard. He was shivering with cold, and he was hungry. I fed him a peanut butter and jelly sandwich. He ate every bit of it and almost licked off my hand too!" Faye looked pleadingly at Roxie. "Please don't tell Mom and Dad I have it! Please please please please *please*."

Roxie sighed. Faye was not going to part with the puppy without a fight. Mom and Dad would have to deal with it—she couldn't. "I won't tell. But you know they'll find out. It would be better if you just showed them the puppy."

"No way! They'd make me give it back!"

"Think how sad the owner must feel, Faye."

"I would feel sad too if I didn't get to keep him. You can't make me give him up by making me feel guilty."

Roxie chuckled before she could stop herself. Faye was very smart for her age. "All right." Faye was sometimes too smart for her own good. Dad said it was from being raised in a family with older kids.

Faye kissed the puppy. "It's only right that I

have a puppy of my own. I call him Cuddles." Faye cuddled the puppy close while she smiled up at Roxie. "See? He's sooo cuddly!"

"He *is* cute, but you'll have to tell Mom and Dad you have him sometime."

"I know—just not yet. I want to enjoy him a while without being scolded by Mom and Dad." Faye buried her face in the puppy's furry back and giggled. "You're the cutest little puppy I've ever seen. I love you, Cuddles."

Roxie slowly walked to her room. She should've stayed at the mall where she didn't have to worry about anything.

She thought about that again the next morning when she heard Lacy crying in her bedroom. She was seventeen, a junior in high school, and worked at Markee's Department Store part-time. Ever since Valentine Day she'd been acting funny, but she wouldn't tell Roxie what was wrong. Lacy kept her feelings and her problems to herself. Mom and Dad worried about her a lot, and that made Roxie worry too. She knew she wasn't supposed to worry, but she hadn't quite learned how not to. She knew the Bible said to cast her cares on Jesus because He cared for her, but she didn't know how to do that. Hannah had said to pray for the answer, and then each time she thought about it, to remember that she'd already prayed and that Jesus was taking care of it. That was easier to say than to do! Hannah said it got easier with practice. Hannah and her family had been Christians a lot longer than Roxie and her family.

Slowly Roxie dressed for church in her blue skirt and long-sleeved, flowered sweater. Should she knock on Lacy's door and ask her what was wrong? Roxie brushed her hair and sprayed it so it would stay back off her forehead. She wrinkled her nose at the smell as she pushed her stocking feet into her dress shoes.

Taking a deep breath, Roxie walked to Lacy's closed door and knocked.

"What?" Lacy asked sharply.

"It's me. Can I come in?"

"I guess." Lacy unlocked her door and opened it. Her eyes were red-rimmed, and the end of her nose was pink. She wore a black skirt and a pink and black sweater. Her long, auburn hair hung down on her back and over her slim shoulders.

"I heard you crying." Roxie swallowed hard. "Can I help?"

"Yeah, sure." Lacy rolled her eyes. "How could *you* help?"

Roxie shrugged. She felt sooo helpless! "I don't know. But I want you to feel better. I want you to be happy."

"Well, there's nothing you can do. Let's go downstairs."

Roxie didn't move. "Did Dan Harland break up with you?"

"I don't want to talk about it." Lacy brushed past Roxie and hurried down the hall.

Roxie sighed heavily. She'd loved Dan, but he had only loved Lacy. Was it possible they weren't going together now? Why wouldn't Lacy say?

Roxie glanced around the bedroom. It smelled like perfume, and it looked like Lacy's whole closet was dumped on her bed. Sometimes Lacy didn't clean her room for a week at a time. With a tired sigh Roxie hurried after Lacy, then stopped at Faye's room. Roxie peeked inside. Faye wasn't there. Was the puppy? Roxie checked Faye's closet, but the puppy wasn't there either. Where had Faye hidden Cuddles? Roxie lifted the toy box lid. It was full of toys. Where was the dog? Roxie shrugged. It wasn't her problem, so why worry about it?

Downstairs she slipped on her Sunday coat and then opened the basement door to listen for Cuddles. The only sound she heard was Dad calling from outdoors for her to hurry. The others were already heading for the station wagon Dad had backed out of the garage.

Roxie clicked the basement door shut and rushed outdoors, pulling the back door tight behind her. Cold wind ruffled her hair and turned her cheeks pink. She saw the Shigwams pulling out of their driveway. Hannah waved, and Roxie lifted her hand. Exhaust swirled out of the tailpipe of the car and drifted up into the gray sky.

Roxie slipped into the backseat beside Faye. Lacy and Eli sat on the other side of Faye and didn't look at Roxie. She sank back as Dad backed out of the driveway. She closed her eyes and tried to forget the problems she knew others in her family were struggling with. None of them wanted her help, so why should she worry? But she did anyway.

Several minutes later Roxie walked into her Sunday school class. The Best Friends had agreed that whoever got there first would save seats for the others. Ten kids already sat talking and laughing while they waited for class to begin. The room was square, with rows of chairs facing the front. Just then the sun peeked through the clouds and shone through three long windows onto the spot where the teacher stood.

Chelsea McCrea walked in with Kathy Aber. Chelsea's long, bright red hair brightened the room even more than the sun. Kathy touched her shoulder-length, natural-blonde curls that often upset her because she couldn't get anything but a long-toothed pick through them. They stopped on either side of Roxie. "Hi," they said at the same time. Roxie wanted to grab them both by their arms and hang on tight, but she walked to a chair and sat down between them. They saved two chairs next to Kathy for Hannah and Colin.

"Can we get together this afternoon?" Roxie whispered.

Chelsea shook her head. "We're going to visit friends Dad made at work." Her dad had been transferred by Benson's Electronics from Oklahoma to their Grand Rapids office, so he was eager to make friends. "I really don't want to go since the people don't have kids my age."

Kathy leaned close to Roxie. "We're having company for the day—Dad's boss and his family." Kathy's dad was the head musician on a Christian TV talk show hosted by Ralph Gentry. "I still get a little nervous being around Dad's famous boss."

Roxie's heart sank. She couldn't be home all day with Eli's secret heavy on her mind, or Faye's either. Roxie looked unseeingly down at the Bible in her hand. Maybe she'd go to the mall again. It was open until 6. At the mall she wouldn't have to think about anything but shopping.

Hannah hurried in with Colin and quickly sat down. Hannah smiled at the Best Friends and said hi. Colin smiled too. It made the girls feel good to see him smile. Before accepting Jesus as his Savior, he'd not smiled once because he lived in such fear of aliens taking over the world. Roxie noticed that he did indeed have a big nose. She frowned. There were much worse things than a big nose.

Just then Marsha Tompert called the class to order and opened with prayer.

Roxie listened to her pray and relaxed for the first time since yesterday.

"We're talking about trusting God today," Marsha said as she pushed back her dark hair, then opened her Bible. "People we love can sometimes fail us, but God never does."

Roxie thought about Eli, and the familiar knot tightened in her stomach. Eli had certainly failed himself and her, as well as the entire family.

"Proverbs 3:5 says, 'Trust in the Lord with all your heart and lean not on your own understanding.'" Marsha glanced around the room at the quiet boys and girls. "Often we look at circumstances around us, and we get scared. It's important to look at the Lord and put our trust in Him. He's promised to be with us always and to take care of us. We can trust Him to help us in any situation."

Roxie listened for a while, but found her mind drifting back to what Eli was planning to do. Maybe she should try to talk to him again. Maybe she could change his mind.

After church Roxie said good-bye to the Best Friends and hurried to the car to talk to Eli alone. Lacy was sitting in the backseat with her face covered with both hands. Eli wasn't there.

Roxie hesitated, then slipped into the backseat and closed the door. "Lacy, what's wrong?" she asked softly.

"Leave me alone," Lacy muttered from behind her hands.

Roxie bit her lip. The words hurt her feelings.

Why couldn't Lacy understand that she honestly wanted to help? Roxie sat silently for a while. Outdoors kids shouted and laughed. Finally Roxie said, "Where's Eli?"

Lacy lifted her head and took a long, shuddering breath. "He went home with someone else—a guy named Nate Irwin. I heard him talk to dad about it."

Roxie's heart sank. Nate Irwin!

Lacy frowned. "What's wrong?"

"I think Eli's in trouble."

Lacy groaned. "What else can go wrong in this family?"

"What do you mean by that?" Roxie asked sharply.

"Nothing!" Lacy brushed at her tears. "Don't you dare say a word to Mom and Dad about me crying! I want to work this out by myself! I'm not a baby anymore."

Roxie felt like crying herself. "Why can't you talk to me? I won't tell Mom and Dad if you don't want me to."

"Stay out of my business, Roxie."

Abruptly Roxie turned away and stared out the window. She couldn't help Eli or Lacy—and not even Faye. Roxie bit her bottom lip to keep it from quivering. What good was she to anybody?

6

Julie Pierson

Forcing all her worries to the back of her mind, Roxie slowly walked toward Penney's where she'd heard sweaters were marked down even more than they were last week. Maybe she could buy one with the money from the carved mouse Grandma had sold. Roxie fingered the money in the front pocket of her jeans as she looked around. The mall wasn't as crowded as on Saturday. Several teens ahead of her were laughing loudly and jostling each other. A woman in a wheelchair frowned at them.

Walking around a man and woman deep in conversation, Roxie thought about the Sunday dinner her family had earlier that day. It had been hard for her to eat the roast, buttered carrots, mashed potatoes, and tossed salad while Mom and Dad chatted. They'd tried to get Lacy to talk, but she'd eaten quickly and had excused herself. A minute later Faye had done the same thing. Roxie had helped clear the table, then hurried to her room. She knew she'd never be able to stay in the quiet house during Sunday naps without bursting wide open. She'd gotten permission to go to the mall. So here she was, walking along and still worrying about the same problems. She had promised herself she wouldn't do that.

"I will not think about Eli or Lacy or Faye," Roxie muttered impatiently.

Once again she pushed the problems away and tried to concentrate on what was on display in the store windows.

Just then Roxie spotted Julie Pierson looking at the window display at Markee's, the department store where Lacy worked. She wasn't working today. Julie seemed tired and bored. She brushed at her eyes. Roxie peered closer. Julie was crying! Roxie hesitated. Should she speak to Julie or leave her alone? Some people—Lacy, for example—hated to be caught crying. Roxie lifted her chin. She couldn't leave Julie alone! She might be the kind of person who was thankful for help.

Roxie stepped to Julie's side. "Hi."

Julie brushed frantically at her tears. "I have something in my eyes . . . Dust or something."

Roxie frowned. "I already know you're crying."

Flushing, Julie turned away.

"Can I help? I might be able to, you know."

"You won't." Julie pulled a tissue from the

pocket of her jeans and blew her nose, then flipped back her long, blonde hair. "How come you're here again today?"

Roxie's heart jerked. "I didn't want to stay home."

"What about your friends?"

"They're busy this afternoon." Roxie forced a smile. "What about you?"

"I hate being home alone."

"Does that happen often?"

Julie nodded. "All the time."

Roxie couldn't imagine being home alone *all* the time. That would be kind of scary.

Julie glanced around to make sure nobody was listening. "I get scared being all by myself."

"Where are your parents?"

Julie shrugged. "They both work, and they love to go to fun places together too, so they're gone most of the time."

"Don't they know you're afraid to be alone?"

"They never asked."

"Why don't you tell them?"

Julie picked at her thumbnail. "They wouldn't care. They don't . . . they don't like me much."

Roxie's brows shot up her forehead. "But they're your mom and dad. They have to care!"

"Who says so?"

Roxie gasped. How would she feel if Mom and Dad didn't like her? "I don't know what to say."

"That's okay."

Roxie took a deep breath. This was too hard for her to deal with. "Shall we shop?"

"Sure. It's my life." Julie's voice was hard. She didn't sound very happy at all.

"Do you really come here so you don't have to be home alone?"

Julie barely nodded. "How about you?"

Roxie was quiet as they walked past two stores. "I came to get away from a few . . . secrets I know and can't tell."

"What kind of secrets?"

Roxie shrugged. Several kids walked past eating popcorn. The smell filled the air for a few seconds, then was gone. "Secrets I know about my brother and sister and promised not to tell to our mom and dad."

"Oh. I never had that problem. I'm an only child, you know." Julie flipped back her hair. "How I wish I had brothers and sisters! I wouldn't care how much trouble they'd be. It's sooo lonely being the only child!"

Just then Roxie spotted Eli standing with Nate Irwin. She caught Julie's arm and stopped her short. "There's my brother!"

"Where?"

"Standing just outside Penney's doorway . . . with an African-American—Nate Irwin."

"Oh yeah. I see them." Julie frowned thoughtfully. "I've seen Nate Irwin before."

"Probably on the six o'clock news," Roxie muttered.

"I remember! He came to our house to ask if I'd seen anything when the house across the street was burglarized."

Roxie shivered and pulled Julie out of sight behind a tall plant. "You mean Nate robbed somebody's house, then asked you if you'd seen anything?"

Julie frowned. "What are you talking about? He was investigating the robbery."

"What do you mean, 'investigating'?"

"He was the policeman investigating it."

Roxie's face turned ashen. "No, Julie. Nate's a high school student. He robbed a convenience store, and now he's trying to get Eli to be one of his accomplices!"

"Are you sure?"

"Very sure." Shivers ran up and down Roxie's spine. "Nate probably was checking your house out so he could rob it. He only pretended to be a policeman."

Julie's eyes widened in alarm. "No! Oh, that's terrible!"

"Let's follow them and see what they're going to do." Roxie shivered. Did she think she was some kind of super-sleuth? Hannah was the one who liked to solve mysteries. But she wasn't here now.

Julie giggled. "And I thought today was going to be just another boring day! This'll be fun."

Roxie tried to look at it that way, but she couldn't. It was frightening to think of what Eli could be getting himself into. Eli was her brother, and he was headed for trouble. She was going to help him even if he didn't want her help.

Eli and Nate talked a minute longer, then walked away from the store and on down the hall. Roxie gripped Julie's arm and tugged her along in pursuit of the two boys.

"We should disguise ourselves," Julie whispered.

Roxie stopped abruptly. "You're right! If Eli saw me following him, he'd really be mad." Roxie frowned. "How can we disguise ourselves?"

"Wigs . . . Dark glasses . . . I don't know."

Roxie watched Eli and Nate getting farther away. "We don't have time to get anything. Hurry, before we lose them." She rushed around several women.

Running beside Roxie, Julie laughed right out loud. She hadn't had this much excitement ever.

Suddenly Roxie stopped. At the crosswalk Eli walked one way and Nate another. "Who should we follow?"

"You go after Eli, and I'll go after Nate." Julie rushed after Nate before Roxie could agree or disagree with the plan.

Roxie took a deep breath and shifted her jacket

to her other arm. Eli would really yell at her if he knew she was following him. She lifted her chin and squared her shoulders. So what? She had to do something, didn't she? She was his sister, after all.

With her heart lodged in her throat, Roxie hurried after Eli. He stopped at the food station, looked around as if he were searching for someone, then hurried to a table where two boys his age were sitting. Roxie ducked behind a tall leafy plant and watched. If only she could get close enough to listen! She studied the boys carefully so she'd know them again when she saw them. Maybe she could look in Lacy's high school yearbook to learn who they were.

Did she dare walk right out into the open? Eli's back was to her. If he saw her, he'd have no idea she'd followed him. He'd think she just happened to be there. Or would he? Her mouth felt dust-dry, and for a minute she couldn't move. Finally she walked away from the security of the plant and out into the area where the tables stood. She got as close as she could before her legs grew too weak to support her. She sank down onto a chair and leaned on the table to try to hear the boys. She scowled with irritation. It was too noisy to hear them!

Just then someone gripped her arm. She jumped and stifled a scream, then looked up to find Julie standing there.

"I'm back," Julie whispered as she sat down. "What about Nate?"

70

"He walked to his car and drove away, so I came to find you." Julie narrowed her eyes as she looked at the boys sitting with Eli. "Do you know those guys?"

Roxie shook her head. "Do you?"

"No. We're not close enough to hear them." Julie's eyes lit up. "I could sit at the table closest to them and listen to them. They don't know me and wouldn't think a thing about me being there."

Roxie's stomach fluttered. "I don't know . . ."

"It'll work. You wait back behind the plant, and I'll get back to you as soon as I can." Julie hurried away before Roxie could stop her.

Roxie reluctantly walked back to the plant and stood behind it. Her nerves tingled as Julie sat at a table beside Eli and the boys. Finally the boys walked away, leaving Eli alone. Julie hurried over to Roxie. "Well?" Roxie said.

"They were talking about school and cars."

"That's it?"

Julie sighed heavily and nodded. "I'm sorry."

"That's all right. We tried." Roxie bit her bottom lip and tried to think of what to do next.

"Look!" Julie gripped Roxie's arm and pointed. "A different boy is sitting down with Eli!"

Roxie shivered. "Go listen again . . . Hurry!" Roxie studied the boy so she'd recognize him if she ever saw him again.

Julie rushed around the tables and dropped

down next to the table where Eli sat. She strained to hear what they were talking about, but she only caught a couple of words that didn't make sense at all. When Eli and the boy walked away, Julie hurried back to Roxie.

"What?" Roxie asked in a tight voice.

"Nothing. I couldn't hear them. Sorry."

"Let's follow Eli again." Trembling, Roxie hurried after Eli. He walked straight to an exit. Roxie hesitated, then hurried after him. He looked deep in thought as he walked across the parking lot. Suddenly she stopped. "He's going home, I think."

Julie felt disappointed. She'd been all set for more excitement. "Are you going to follow him?"

"My bike's on the other side of the mall." Roxie and Julie slowly walked back the way they'd come. Inside the mall Roxie turned to Julie. "I guess I'll go home. Will you be all right?"

Julie shrugged.

"Want to come to my house for a while?"

Julie shook her head. "I guess I'll go home too." But after what Roxie had said about Nate, Julie didn't really want to go home yet. But she didn't want Roxie to feel obligated to help her just because she felt sorry for her either. "See you tomorrow."

"Sure." Roxie started away, then stopped. "Julie, please don't say anything to anyone about Eli or about us following him. Okay?"

"I won't. Be sure to let me know what you find out."

"I will if I can." Roxie hurried away, her head spinning. What if she found out something so terrible she wouldn't want to tell anyone—not even the Best Friends?

7

Sunday Night

Easing open Faye's bedroom door, Roxie slipped inside, then wrinkled her nose. The foul odor almost took her breath away. "Faye! It stinks in here!"

Faye squealed and tried to hide Cuddles. Her eyes wide in alarm, she backed up against her closet door with Cuddles in her arms. "Roxie, you can't just sneak in here!"

"I can too!" Roxie shook her finger at Faye. Faye's eyes looked huge in her pale face. "Did you tell Mom and Dad about the puppy?"

Faye hung her head and whispered, "No."

"They'll smell him as soon as they open the door. Didn't you take the puppy outside so he wouldn't go on your floor?"

Shivering, Faye pointed to a pile of dog manure in the corner of her bedroom. "I wanted to clean it up, but I didn't know what to do."

Holding her nose, Roxie hurried to the bathroom and pulled off several sheets of toilet paper. She slipped back into Faye's room and gingerly picked up the pile. Her stomach lurched, and she thought she was going to throw up. Sticking her hand and arm way out in front of her, she carried the manure to the toilet and flushed it down. Shivering and making a face, she scrubbed her hands with plenty of hot water and soap. Would she ever get rid of the smell?

When she got back to Faye's room, Roxie opened the window to let in fresh air. Chilly wind blew in and pushed away the disgusting smell. Roxie closed the window and turned to Faye, who was now sitting on the floor with Cuddles on her lap. "I won't clean up any messes again, Faye! I mean it! Tell Mom and Dad about Cuddles."

Giant tears welled up in Faye's eyes. "I love Cuddles."

"I know, but he doesn't belong to you, so you have to tell Mom and Dad about him."

"I promise to take him outside so he won't have another accident in here. I promise, I promise, I promise!"

"Faye, you can't promise that. You'll be in preschool tomorrow. What will happen while you're gone?"

With her head against Cuddles Faye thought for a long time. Finally she looked up at Roxie. "I'll put him in the basement."

Roxie sighed heavily. She wished Faye could

keep the puppy, but that was impossible. Dad and Mom had said over and over that they couldn't have a dog. They didn't like dogs in the house, and they didn't want a dog running around the neighborhood causing trouble like Gracie did. "You have to tell them, Faye. You know that."

"I can't, Roxie." Faye held Cuddles closer. "I love him too much."

Roxie started to turn away, then knelt on the floor beside Faye and took her and the puppy in her arms. Roxie held them for a long time. Faye sniffed hard to keep from crying. Cuddles licked Roxie's cheek. Roxie sat back on her heels and brushed strands of damp hair from Faye's face. "I won't tell, but you will."

"No, I won't," Faye whispered, shaking her head until her ponytails whipped across her face and Cuddles.

"You can't disobey Mom and Dad."

"I can if I want!" But Faye didn't sound very sure of herself.

Roxie patted Cuddles on the head. "And you sure can't steal someone's puppy."

"I didn't steal him." Faye puckered up her face to cry. "He was right in the yard. That's not stealing."

"Taking something that doesn't belong to you is stealing." That made Roxie think about Eli, and she jumped up, her stomach a cold, tight ball. "Take

Cuddles downstairs right now and show him to Mom and Dad."

Faye pressed her lips tightly together and looked very stubborn.

Roxie walked out and closed Faye's door, then hurried to Eli's room. She had to talk to him before she lost her nerve again. The door was half open. She knocked, and that made the door open further. Eli was sitting at his desk deep in thought. He wore a white T-shirt and jeans. His feet were bare. "Eli . . ." He didn't answer. She licked her dry lips. "Eli . . ." she said a little more loudly.

He jumped and turned his head. "Hi." He didn't sound mad, but he didn't sound like he wanted to talk either.

She managed to smile as she walked in. "What did you do today?" As if she didn't know!

He shrugged. "This and that. Hung out at the mall a while. Why?"

"I just wondered." How she wanted to tell him she'd seen him! "Want to play a game?"

"Not now. I have schoolwork." He opened a book on his desk and started reading it.

Her heart turned over. "Nate Irwin robbed a convenience store, you know."

Eli glared at Roxie. "Get out of here!"

She felt like she was going to burst into tears, but she wouldn't let herself. "You can't hang out with him without getting a bad reputation."

Eli shrugged. "So?"

Tears blurred her vision, and she walked out without another word. What a wimp she was! Why couldn't she tell him what she'd seen and ask him what was going on?

She thought about the boys he'd met at the mall and remembered she wanted to look in Lacy's yearbook to learn their names. She hurried to Lacy's room and knocked. "Lacy, it's me. Can I come in?"

"Why?"

"I want to see your yearbook."

Lacy jerked open the door a crack and thrust the book into Roxie's hand. "Don't ruin it!"

"I won't." Before Roxie could say another word, Lacy closed her door and locked it. Roxie sighed heavily and hurried to her room. She flung herself across her bed on her stomach and looked through the book for Nate Irwin. Shivers tingled up and down her spine. Would she find Nate and the other boys she'd seen with Eli in the yearbook?

She ran her finger along the photos, then stopped, barely breathing. It was the boy who'd stopped at Eli's table last! His name was Wayne Sinclair. He was short and overweight with brown hair that needed trimming and brown eyes. He wasn't smiling in the picture, and he hadn't smiled at the mall. "Wayne Sinclair." Roxie jumped up and rushed across the room to her desk. She wrote his name and description on a paper. "Wayne Sinclair, what kind of boy are you?"

Roxie studied Wayne a long time, then looked for the other boys. She spotted another one, and her heart leaped. "Tad Woodley." Just saying his name hurt her throat. She quickly jotted his name below Wayne's.

Sitting at the desk, she flipped through the pages of the yearbook again. She couldn't find Nate or the other boy. She started at the front of the book and looked again, then again. Finally she found the other boy in a snapshot toward the back of the book. But his name wasn't listed. Roxie's heart sank. She had to know his name! Maybe Lacy knew his name.

Roxie grabbed the yearbook and ran to Lacy's door. Roxie knocked three sharp raps. "Lacy, I need to ask you something."

Lacy jerked open the door. For once her eyes weren't red-rimmed. She had a book in her hand. "What is it this time?"

Roxie pushed the yearbook at Lacy. "Who is this boy?"

Lacy peered at the snapshot. "Gabe Pressley. Why?"

"What's he like?"

Lacy shrugged. "He's okay, I guess. Why?"

"I just wondered." Roxie couldn't tell about her suspicions and give Lacy even more to be upset about. Roxie handed Lacy the yearbook. "Thanks. I was looking for Nate Irwin, but he's not in there."

"He's only been at school a few weeks."

"Oh. Where'd he live before?"

Lacy shrugged. She started to shut the door.

"Wait!"

Lacy frowned, but she left the door open a crack.

"Have you heard anything either good or bad about Nate?"

"No." Lacy closed the door and locked it.

Roxie felt like kicking the door, but she walked to her room. She looked out the window at the streetlights casting their beautiful glow across the snow. She knew the names of the boys Eli had met at the mall, but what should she do now?

■

Her face cold from the wind, Julie Pierson walked home from the mall as slowly as she could. It was dark except for the streetlights when she reached her yard. No light shone from her house, and she knew nobody was home. Her key was in her pocket. She'd carried a house key since she was nine years old. She hesitated at her door. How she hated walking inside! She put the key in the lock but didn't turn it. Shivers trickled down her backbone. What if someone was inside stealing everything in sight? She put her ear to the door and listened. It was quiet inside, but she still couldn't bring herself to turn the key. She frowned. She couldn't just stand outside the house. Anger rushed through her, and she unlocked the door before her courage drained away again. She slipped inside and cocked her head, listening for the slightest sound. She didn't hear anything except the grandmother clock beside her. Taking a deep, steadying breath, she hung her jacket in the closet. The house was warm and smelled of coffee.

The phone rang, shattering the silence. Julie jumped and ran to the kitchen to answer it there. She touched the receiver, then jerked back as if she'd been burned. What if the caller only wanted to see if she was home alone? But what if it was Mom or Dad saying they wouldn't be home until really late?

Julie scooped up the phone and said in a low voice, "Hello."

"Julie?"

It was Roxie. Julie sagged against the counter. "Yes, this is Julie. Hi, Roxie."

"I found those boys in Lacy's yearbook. Wayne Sinclair . . . Tad Woodley . . . Gabe Pressley. Do you know the names?"

"No . . . I don't think so."

"Nate Irwin wasn't in the book. Lacy said he's been in the school only a few weeks."

Julie shivered. "I'm really scared about Nate Irwin pretending to be a policeman. Maybe we should report him."

"That's a great idea. Will you do it?"

"Me? No . . . I'd be too scared."

Roxie was quiet a long time. "Yeah, me too. I guess we can't do anything, can we?"

"I guess not."

Just then Julie heard the back door open and her mom laughing. "My folks are home. I have to go."

Julie hung up and waited for her folks to come into the kitchen. She painted a smile on her face. They didn't like it when she frowned or looked scared. They walked in looking like the perfect couple you'd see on TV. Julie wanted to beg them to notice her—really notice her, but of course they didn't. They were involved in a spirited conversation about someone they'd seen while they were having dessert in a downtown restaurant. At a lull in the conversation Julie said, "Hi."

"Hi." Mom smiled as she took a pitcher of juice out of the refrigerator. "Did you have a pleasant afternoon?"

"Yes. I met my best friends at the mall, and we tried on all kinds of clothes." Julie managed to keep smiling. The lie burned a hole in her tongue. She couldn't very well tell them the truth. They didn't like it when she said she didn't have any friends.

Dad brushed his hand down Julie's arm, and she wanted to lean on him to keep his hand on her longer. She wanted so badly to be held and touched and talked to like girls in other families were.

"I'm glad you have friends," Dad said as he accepted a glass of juice from Mom.

Julie kept her smile glued on. She'd even given names to her friends—Chelsea, Hannah, Roxie, and Kathy. Her folks would never know she'd lied.

Dad sat at the table. "Claire, I forgot to tell you . . ."

"What, Ron?" Mom sat down at the table with them.

Julie started to walk out. They'd already forgotten she was there. Just as she started out the door she heard Dad say something about another break-in. She hurried back into the kitchen and leaned weakly against the counter.

Dad sipped his juice, wiped his mouth with a napkin, then set the glass on the table. "I heard a couple of policemen talking at the courthouse about a break-in on Washington and Elm. Same things were taken as at the other houses—TV, VCR, sound system, and cash."

Julie thought about Dad's sophisticated sound system in the living room, and she trembled. Would the thieves know about the sound system and break in to get it?

"I'm telling you, nobody better try to get in my house!" Dad tapped his chest with his open hands.

Mom laughed. "I don't think the thief checks to see who lives where. He wouldn't know he'd be up against *you*." She leaned toward him and kissed him.

Julie walked out. She couldn't watch them or listen to them. They didn't even think for a moment about her being home alone. They didn't make sure she was safe. They wouldn't even notice if she was kidnapped or if she ran away.

With a sob she covered her face with her hands.

8

No School

Roxie finished her breakfast Monday morning just as the phone rang. Mom answered it, listened a while, then hung up. Roxie waited, her eyes on Mom.

"Well, you have a surprise, Roxie." Mom smiled as she handed Faye a napkin. "There's something wrong with the furnace at the middle school, so you don't have school today."

"No!" Roxie's heart sank. She'd planned to ask the Best Friends to help her learn about the boys she'd seen with Eli yesterday at the mall. She was going to tell them all about Eli and about the puppy Faye had found. She had the names of the boys in her jeans pocket. She was sure the Best Friends would help her know what to do.

"Do I have to stay home too?" Faye asked in alarm.

"No. Only the middle school is closed." Mom urged Faye toward the door. Eli and Lacy had left several minutes before. "Roxie, I have to take Faye to school, then run some errands. Will you be all right alone?"

"Sure. I'll see what Chelsea and Hannah are doing."

"I won't be back until late this afternoon."

Roxie nodded. "I'll be all right." She thought about Julie. What would she do all day by herself? "Chelsea, Hannah, Kathy, and I have to see Mrs. Murphy about a job she has for us. If we can, we'll see her today."

"Fine. Just leave me a note so I'll know where you are."

"I will." Roxie hugged Mom, then bent down to hug Faye. "Did you tell them?" she whispered in Faye's ear.

Faye shook her head.

Roxie sighed heavily as Faye and Mom left. Roxie decided right then she'd have to find out who the puppy belonged to and let them know he was safe. Maybe when Faye actually met the owner, she'd be able to give up Cuddles.

The phone rang, and Roxie grabbed it. "Hello."

"Hi. It's Chelsea. Great news, huh?"

"I guess. Are we going to see Mrs. Murphy now?"

"Yes. I called her already. Hannah said she could go. I have to call Kathy yet."

85

"I'll be over at your house in a few minutes."
Roxie took a deep breath. "Chel, have you heard if
anyone's missing a little, brown puppy?"

"No. Why?"

"I'll tell you when I see you." Roxie hung up
and ran downstairs to check on Cuddles. Faye had
put him in a cardboard box behind some other
boxes. Roxie peeked into the box, and the puppy
whimpered. He had a bowl of water and one of
food. "Who do you belong to?"

Roxie sighed and ran back upstairs. Maybe the
owner had put an ad in the Lost and Found. Why
hadn't she thought of that before? Roxie found that
day's paper in the kitchen under Dad's chair. She
nervously opened it on the island counter and
checked the ads. She ran her finger down the col-
umn, then stopped when she saw, "LOST PUPPY."
Her heart raced, and she trembled as she read the
description. The description fit the puppy Faye had
hidden in the box in the basement. In fact, the puppy
belonged to Barb Mayhew, Colin's mom! Why
hadn't Colin said anything to any of them?

Roxie groaned. She couldn't call Mrs. Mayhew
because she worked outside the home. Roxie slowly
walked to the closet for her jacket. She'd talk to
Mrs. Mayhew later, then take Faye to talk to her.
Maybe the puppy wouldn't be Mrs. Mayhew's after
all. Roxie stopped at the door and looked back at

the kitchen door. Maybe she could call and leave a message on their answering machine.

Her mouth dry, Roxie hurried to the phone and dialed the Mayhews' number. Colin answered immediately, and Roxie said, "Hi, Colin. This is Roxie Shoulders. How come you're home? Did the furnace go out at your private school too?"

"No. I'm running a bit of a fever, so Mom thought I should stay home and rest."

"Oh." Roxie took a deep breath. "Well, anyway, I just read in the Lost and Found ads that your mom lost a puppy."

Colin was quiet a long time. "We don't have a puppy. Dad says we can't."

"But the ad gives your phone number and your mom's name."

"That's really strange."

"Could she have a puppy without you knowing it?"

"I guess. But why would she?"

Roxie shrugged, then realized Colin couldn't see her shrug over the phone. "I don't know. What time will she be home?"

"Around 4."

"I'd like to see her if I could."

"Sure. Come over just after 4. I'll tell her you're coming."

"Thanks. What are you going to do today since you're not at school?"

"Finish a book I have to write a report on and do some homework. How about you?"

"Some work at Mrs. Murphy's. I'm on my way to Chelsea's now. See ya later." Roxie hung up and hurried outdoors. A chilly wind blew snow across the yard as she ran to Chelsea's. A red pickup slowly drove past, leaving exhaust swirling out behind it.

Just then Hannah ran down her sidewalk and across the street. "Hi," she called, smiling happily.

"Hi. Were you surprised there's no school?"

Hannah nodded as she knocked on Chelsea's door. "It's like another snow day. I guess I'd rather go to school just to keep from getting bored. Going to see Mrs. Murphy will help though."

Giggling, Roxie nudged Hannah. "You could see Colin too. He's home with a fever, though he doesn't feel very sick. He's reading and doing homework."

"I know. He called me a while ago."

Chelsea walked out, zipping her jacket. "Hi. Kathy said she'd meet us there." Mrs. Murphy lived outside The Ravines, so it was easier for Kathy to go right to her house.

Roxie got her bike from the garage. Her heart sank in disappointment that she'd have to wait to tell the Best Friends about Eli and the puppy when they were all together.

Several minutes later they left their bikes leaning against the garage, and Chelsea rang Mrs. Murphy's back doorbell. A short, fat snowman with a big straw hat, a carrot nose, and black button eyes stood nearby. Gospel music drifted out from the one-story white frame house.

Kesha Bronski, Mrs. Murphy's foster daughter, opened the door with a glad cry. Kesha's blonde hair was held back with a wide, gold band. She wore jeans and a navy-blue sweatshirt. "Come on in! I'm sure glad to see you girls. This was going to be a very boring day!"

Roxie stepped in behind Hannah. Warm air wrapped around them along with the smell of freshly baked cinnamon rolls.

Kesha led them to the kitchen where Mrs. Murphy was having a cup of coffee and a roll. She was short and plump and had graying brown hair. Her children were grown up and lived on their own. One of her sons was a teacher at Middle Lake Middle School. She wiped a napkin across her mouth, then smiled at the girls. "I'm glad you could come this morning. Sit down." She pointed to the plate of rolls covered with frosting and nuts. "Help yourselves."

Kesha set small white plates on the table and served the girls. She poured milk for them. While they ate, Mrs. Murphy talked to them about themselves and whatever was new in their lives.

Suddenly Roxie realized Mrs. Murphy knew almost everybody in Middle Lake. She might know the boys on her list in her pocket. Her nerves crackled, and it was hard to sit still.

Finally Mrs. Murphy said, "The job I have for you girls will take time, but it's fun too. I need several dozen cookies baked. I want four different kinds of cookies—chocolate-chip being one of them, of course."

"And peanut butter," Kesha said with a grin. "It's my favorite."

Hannah wiped her mouth. "How about chocolate chocolate-chip?"

"Great!" Mrs. Murphy nodded.

"And sugar cookies!" Chelsea laughed. "I just learned to make them. We can leave them plain or frost them different colors."

Mrs. Murphy got a pencil and pad and jotted down the four kinds of cookies. "List the ingredients we'll need so I can shop. I want to be ready with everything."

Roxie's mind drifted to the problems she was facing as the others named off the ingredients. She was anxious to ask Mrs. Murphy about the four boys. Finally the grocery list was done. Before they started talking about anything else Roxie said, "Mrs. Murphy, do you know a high school boy named Nate Irwin?"

Mrs. Murphy frowned in thought. "I don't believe I do. Why?"

Roxie didn't want to answer Mrs. Murphy yet. "How about Wayne Sinclair?"

Mrs. Murphy nodded. "Sure, I know Wayne.

He's been kind of a troublemaker since elementary school."

Roxie felt the girls staring at her questioningly, but she didn't want to say more yet. "Tad Woodley?"

"I know his mother quite well . . . Priscilla Adgate."

Roxie gasped. They'd built the snow family for her! "I didn't know that!"

"Tad lives with his dad. Priscilla is in her second marriage." Mrs. Murphy shook her head. "That boy is bad news. I'm sure his parents' divorce has a lot to do with it, but it doesn't excuse his actions. He needs a lot of help."

Roxie's stomach knotted painfully. Would Tad be a bad influence on Eli, who was too easily persuaded? "How about Gabe Pressley?"

"Gabe runs with Tad, and they're both in trouble most of the time. Why do you want to know about these boys?" Mrs. Murphy frowned at Roxie.

She flushed and looked down at her icy hands. Finally she lifted her head. She had to tell somebody! "My brother Eli has been hanging out with them."

"I'm sorry to hear that." Mrs. Murphy pursed her lips. "Eli is a fine boy with a good reputation. Could he be trying to help them?"

Roxie ducked her head. How could she answer that without making Eli seem bad?

"Roxie?" Mrs. Murphy asked softly.

Roxie swallowed hard. She could feel the Best

Friends almost bursting with curiosity. She could feel their love and kindness too. "I saw Eli with those boys, and I'm afraid he's going to be persuaded to do something he shouldn't."

"Did you tell your parents?"

Roxie shook her head. "I promised Eli I wouldn't."

"If it's for his good, you should break your word. Making a promise like that wasn't wise. Keeping the promise could be harmful to Eli." Mrs. Murphy reached across the table and patted Roxie's arm. "Think about it. I don't want to tell you what to do. The decision is yours."

"You could find out more about the boys," Hannah said. "I could ask my dad. He hears everything about everybody!"

Roxie's eyes lit up. "All of you ask around about the four boys, and then I'll decide if I should tell my folks."

Kathy pushed a pad of paper toward Roxie. "Write down their names for each of us, and we'll do what we can."

"Thanks!" Roxie wrote the names in her best handwriting and passed them out to the girls.

Later the girls slipped on their jackets while Mrs. Murphy discussed the best time for them to come bake cookies. Finally they decided on Thursday after school.

"Ask your folks if you can eat supper with us."

Mrs. Murphy slipped an arm around Kesha. "We'll make pizza. Kesha has turned into a great pizza baker."

Kesha smiled at Mrs. Murphy, then at the Best Friends. "I use extra cheese."

Roxie couldn't keep her mind on the chatter as they all prepared to leave. Suddenly she had a brilliant idea. She waited until they were on their bikes before she said anything. "I'd like to talk to Mrs. Adgate about Tad. Will you girls go with me?"

"Sure."

Roxie smiled her thanks and led the way back to The Ravines and to Priscilla Adgate's home. The snow family and dog looked as good as they had when the girls first built them.

Just then Stacia King stepped outdoors and called, "Hi, girls. What's up?"

"We came to talk to Mrs. Adgate." Roxie pushed her cold hands down into the pockets of her jacket.

"She's not home. I saw her drive away about fifteen minutes ago."

Roxie kicked a clump of snow in frustration. What should she do now?

9

More Information

Scowling, Roxie walked into the mall. The Best Friends had had to go home before lunch. None of them could have anyone over, so she'd left a note for Mom and tried to call Julie. There was no answer, so she'd come to the mall to keep from exploding. It was easier to forget everything if she shopped. She still had the money from selling the carving.

As she walked, she looked for Julie. She was probably already at the mall. A woman pushed a baby along in a stroller. A man hurried along, his coattails flipping around his legs. The mall looked almost deserted. It smelled like potpourri.

Roxie stopped outside Markee's, the store where Lacy would be working after school today. Roxie looked at the shoes and spring clothes in the window. Maybe she could go to the teen department where Lacy worked and find out if Lacy's being upset so often was about something at work.

Roxie abruptly pushed the thought aside. She was here to forget her troubles, not to try to solve Lacy's!

With a toss of her head Roxie hurried away. She spotted Julie sitting on a bench with her head in her hands. Roxie hesitated. Could she stand to be with Julie and her heartache?

Just then Julie looked up. Her face was white and her eyes full of fear. She saw Roxie and leaped to her feet. "There was another break-in last night—just down the street from us!"

Roxie gasped. Suddenly her legs felt too weak to support her. She dropped to the bench and gripped her jacket with clenched fists. Finally Julie sat down beside her.

"The same things were taken—VCR, TV, sound system, and cash." Julie was so frightened, she didn't think she could stay in her house alone ever again.

Roxie immediately thought about Eli. She remembered that he was home last night—unless he'd sneaked out after everyone was asleep. The thought sent a stab of pain through her heart. How could she find out if Eli had been home all night? She pushed the thought aside. Right now she wanted to find out everything Julie knew. "Did the police catch anybody?"

Julie shook her head. "Dad said they suspect some teenage boys that a neighbor man, Mr.

Blessman, saw hanging out around the house. He told dad what the boys looked like." Julie gripped Roxie's arm. "Two of the boys sound like the ones we saw talking to your brother yesterday!"

Roxie trembled and almost dropped her jacket. She pulled the list from her pocket and unfolded the paper with unsteady hands. "I found out their names from Lacy's yearbook."

Julie read the list. "How can we find out if these boys are guilty or innocent?"

"We can show their pictures to Mr. Blessman." Roxie could barely get the words out.

"Your brother's too?" Julie asked in astonishment.

Roxie shivered. "No. It would be too awful if Mr. Blessman recognized him." Just thinking about that sent prickles of fear over her. What would she do if Eli had helped the boys break into the house? Maybe she *should* show Mr. Blessman Eli's photo.

"Mr. Blessman stayed home from work today." Julie pushed the paper back into Roxie's hand. "Let's go talk to him now."

"Now?"

"While he still remembers what the boys look like."

Roxie's nerves tightened. "I'll have to get a yearbook first." But she didn't move. She couldn't find the strength. Maybe it would be better not to know whom Mr. Blessman had seen.

"I could go to your house with you to get the yearbook."

Roxie nodded but still didn't move.

"What's wrong?"

"What if I find out Eli did break into that house?" The words made her throat ache.

With her eyes full of sympathy, Julie patted Roxie's arm. "Wouldn't you rather know the truth? Maybe Eli's not guilty. Maybe you've been worrying for nothing."

Maybe she had! Roxie pushed herself up. "Let's do it!"

■

Much later Roxie gripped Lacy's yearbook as Julie knocked on Mr. Blessman's door.

He opened the door with a cup of coffee in his large hand. He stood well over six feet tall and looked like a giant bear in his fuzzy, brown sweater. He smiled. "Yes? Oh, hi, Julie."

"Hi, Mr. Blessman," Julie said. "This is Roxie, my friend. Could we show you some pictures from this yearbook to see if these are the guys who robbed the house over there?"

"Sure. Come on in out of the cold." He stepped aside so they could enter.

Her face as white as the pages in the yearbook, Roxie opened the yearbook and pointed to Eli. She wanted to get that settled immediately before she fainted right on Mr. Blessman's flowered carpet.

Mr. Blessman peered at the girls, then frowned down at the photo. He studied it for a long time. "Could be. I'm not sure."

Roxie trembled. Could be? No! Never! She flipped to Wayne Sinclair. "How about him?"

"It's hard to tell."

Roxie's heart sank, but she showed him Tad Woodley's photo anyway. "Him?"

"Yes. I believe so." Mr. Blessman nodded.

Roxie and Julie looked at each other in triumph.

"I wouldn't swear to it, but this boy sure looks like the one I caught a look at the longest."

Roxie weakly turned to the back of the book to Gabe Pressley.

"I know that boy! That's Gabe Pressley. He delivered the paper to me last year. I don't think he was there last night."

"Were they all white, or was a black boy with them?" Julie asked.

"I don't know." Mr. Blessman looked sharply at the girls. "What's going on? You girls playing detective?"

They nodded. "But we won't get in the policemen's way," Roxie said quickly.

"If the thieves know what you're doing, you could be in danger from them."

The girls exchanged startled looks. They hadn't

thought about that. They quickly said good-bye and hurried to their bikes.

Roxie looked at her watch. "I have to get home. I'd ask you to go with me, but I'm not allowed to have anyone over when Mom's not home. You could go with me in case she is home."

Julie shook her head. "I'll probably go back to the mall."

"Julie, tell your mom and dad how you feel about being home alone. They'll understand."

Julie shook her head. "They'll like me even less if I do. No . . . I can't tell them." She forced a smile. "Don't worry about me, Roxie. I'll be all right. See you in school." She rode away with her blonde hair streaming out behind her.

Roxie sighed and rode home. Nobody was there, but Mom had left a note on the table saying she and Faye would be back by 5. Roxie left the yearbook in Lacy's room, then hurried to Colin's house to talk to his mom. Roxie almost changed her mind and thought about running back home, but she reversed her spin and knocked. She could at least help Faye by finding out about the puppy.

Colin opened the door and whispered, "Mom got really nervous when I told her you were coming to talk to her about the puppy. I don't know what's going on. Maybe she bought it as a surprise for me, so I won't stay with you when you talk to her."

"Okay." Roxie nodded as she slipped off her

jacket and gave it to Colin to hang in the closet. She would've been nervous about talking to Barb Mayhew, but her mind was full of Eli and his problems. Faye and the puppy were much easier to deal with.

"She's in the living room." Colin led the way.

Barb Mayhew pushed herself up from the sofa as Colin introduced her to Roxie. Barb Mayhew had a medium build and large blue eyes, pale skin, and light brown hair. She was wearing black slacks, low-heeled black leather shoes, and a light blue blouse with a flowered vest. She smiled nervously at Roxie.

"Colin said you want to talk to me about a puppy."

Roxie nodded.

"I'll see you later." Smiling, Colin hurried away.

Barb sat down and motioned for Roxie to do the same.

"My little sister Faye found a puppy in our backyard. She's been praying for a puppy, so she thought it was all right for her to keep it. I told her it wasn't. My folks don't know she has it. I think it's the puppy you lost."

Barb laced her fingers together and darted a look toward the door, then looked back at Roxie. "This is very embarrassing."

Roxie frowned slightly. "Why?"

"I got the puppy against my husband's wishes,

so when he disappeared, I was thankful. I put the ad in the paper because I didn't want him running around lost and maybe getting hurt or starving. Maybe your little sister could keep the puppy."

"Our dad doesn't want us to have a puppy."

"I'm sorry to hear that."

"Faye is keeping Cuddles hidden." Roxie giggled self-consciously. "Faye named the puppy Cuddles because he's so cuddly."

Barb smiled. "He *is* cuddly!"

"I'd like you to talk to Faye about Cuddles. She can't keep a puppy that doesn't belong to her. She knows that, and it's making her feel sooo guilty. Of course, she tries to hide her guilt."

"I'm sorry. Of course I'll talk to her. We'll work something out."

"Thank you!"

"My husband is against us having a puppy, but I'll talk to him." Barb cleared her throat and suddenly looked very determined. "Maybe there's a way we can share Cuddles with Faye."

"That would be really nice." Roxie jumped up. She wished all her problems could be solved so easily.

Several minutes later Roxie stood outside her house. The sun felt warm on her skin. Water dripped from the tips of the icicles hanging on the eaves. Faye's problem was practically solved. Could she do the same for Lacy and Eli? She had to try. She glanced at her watch. Lacy was at work. Roxie ran to her bike. She'd go to Markee's and see Lacy at work even if she got mad. Roxie pedaled toward the mall. Maybe she could learn why Lacy was so upset. If it wasn't something at work, then she'd talk to Lacy's special friend Dan Harland—if she could find the courage.

At the mall Roxie hesitated at the bottom of the escalator. The smells of perfume and potpourri filled the air. Shoppers talked and laughed and hurried onto the moving stairway. Roxie took a deep breath and stepped onto the stairs. Her stomach dipped as she reached the top and stepped off. Too bad Julie wasn't with her to give her support.

She stopped outside the teen department where Lacy worked. Spring clothes brightened the area. Teens laughed and talked as they looked at all the goods.

Just then Roxie spotted Mrs. Turner, Lacy's supervisor. She was talking to a dark-haired girl. Roxie walked closer to Mrs. Turner as the girl was saying, "I finished hanging the blouses."

"Thank you."

Roxie looked around for Lacy and finally spotted her near the purses. Roxie started toward her just as she heard the girl say, "Lacy got in late again today."

"I'll deal with Lacy, Peggy."

"I was only trying to help. She was rude to a customer too."

Roxie pressed her lips tightly together. How dare this Peggy say bad things about Lacy! Once again Roxie started to walk away, but she stopped when she heard Peggy say, "Mrs. Turner, I know I saw Lacy stealing a pair of socks a while ago."

Roxie's temper shot through the top of the building. How dare Peggy tell lies about Lacy! Lacy would never ever steal! Roxie wanted to tell Peggy just what she thought of her, but she bit back the sharp words. She didn't want to make it any worse on Lacy than it already was.

Slowly Roxie walked over to Lacy. "Hi."

Lacy smiled in surprise. "Hi. I didn't see you come in."

"I thought I'd see how you are." Roxie didn't know how to tell Lacy what Peggy had said.

"I'm okay, I guess."

"I'll see you at home later."

"Okay."

Tears pricked Roxie's eyes, but she quickly blinked them away. She didn't want to cry. "Are you okay, Lacy?"

She shrugged. "I guess."

"How's your job?"

"Fine." Tears welled up in Lacy's eyes, and she quickly looked away. "You better leave before I get in trouble."

Roxie nodded. She wanted to say something to

make Lacy feel better, but she didn't know what to say. "See you later."

"Yeah."

Roxie forced a smile and walked away. Should she tell Lacy what she'd heard Peggy say? But Lacy might not want to know. Roxie didn't know what she should do.

Slowly Roxie walked to her bike and pedaled home. Lacy's problem suddenly seemed more complicated to Roxie than before. Was there some way she could help Lacy?

10

Help

Roxie waited until Eli was in his bedroom, then ran to his door. She knocked. "I'm coming in." She pushed open the door, stepped inside the room, and closed the door behind her. It was hard to breathe and harder still to stand on her shaky legs. She looked at Eli accusingly. "There was another break-in last night."

"I heard." He set his books in a pile beside his computer.

"Were you there?"

His face white, Eli whipped around and gripped her arms. His eyes flashed behind his glasses. "Leave me alone! I told you to stay out of my business!"

His anger alarmed her, but she didn't turn away. "I showed your picture to Mr. Blessman. He lives near the house that was broken into last night."

"What? . . . How could you?" Eli forced himself to lower his voice.

"He was pretty sure Tad Woodley was one of the boys."

"Roxie!" Eli pushed his nose down to hers. His breath smelled like dill pickles. "What have you done?"

"I want to keep you from doing something wrong!"

"You don't know what you've done! You have no idea!" He shook her, then abruptly set her free. He jabbed his fingers through his dark hair. "You might have ruined everything! You might have ruined me!"

Roxie cried out and cringed away from Eli. "Ruined you? By trying to get you away from boys with bad reputations?"

"Yes." Eli reached around her and opened the door. "Get out! And don't stick your nose in my business again!"

Bursting into tears, Roxie ran from the room.

Eli watched until she shut her door, then hurried to the phone in the hall outside Lacy's room. His breathing ragged, he punched the numbers. When Nate answered, Eli said, "Nate, I think my sister ruined everything. We'd better talk."

With her ear pressed against the door, Roxie could just hear what Eli was saying. What could he mean?

"I'll wait for you inside our garage . . . At midnight."

Her stomach a solid knot, Roxie bit her lip. Could she eavesdrop on Eli and Nate? Yes, she could, if it would help her brother. She heard Eli go back to his room. Stealthily she opened her door and peeked out. Smells of dinner they'd finished a few minutes before floated up the stairs. Just then Faye stuck her head out the door. She looked ready to cry. She saw Roxie and quickly ducked back into her room.

Roxie ran to Faye's room and slipped inside just in time to see her hide Cuddles in the closet.

Faye looked back at Roxie with a gasp.

"It's all right, Faye," Roxie said softly. "I came to help you."

"You did?"

"Yes."

Faye burst into tears and flung herself against Roxie and hung on tight.

Roxie held Faye for a long time, then wiped away her tears. "I talked to Cuddles's owner today. I said I'd take you to talk to her too."

Faye knuckled her eyes. "Does she hate me for taking her puppy?"

"No." Roxie kissed Faye's flushed cheek. "But you know you were wrong to do it."

"Yes," she whispered. "I tried not to feel wrong, but I did anyway."

"Jesus will forgive you if you ask Him to."

Faye sighed in great relief. "I was sooo afraid He wouldn't!"

Roxie prayed with Faye right then. A few minutes later they walked out of the room with Cuddles wrapped in a blanket. After they talked to Barb Mayhew, they'd tell Mom and Dad all about Cuddles.

Outdoors the sun was still shining, but a cold wind was blowing. Cuddles whimpered as he poked his nose out of the blanket.

Standing in front of the Mayhews' house, Faye's eyes filled with tears again. "I can't survive without Cuddles, Roxie!"

"Yes, you can. Remember, Jesus is always with you to help you."

"I know." Faye forced back her tears and nodded as Roxie knocked on the door.

Barb Mayhew answered and stepped quickly outside, shivering in the cold without a coat on. "You brought Cuddles," she said with a low, pleased laugh.

Faye held him out to Barb. "I'm sorry I took him. He was in my yard, so I thought God had sent him to me." Faye blushed. "I guess I didn't *really* think that. I was only hoping it was true."

Barb smiled at Faye. "It took a lot of courage for you to bring Cuddles back. Thank you."

"You're welcome." Faye's voice quivered, but she didn't cry.

Roxie caught Faye's hand and held it firmly to comfort her.

Barb reached for the doorknob. "I have to show Cuddles to my husband. Tomorrow afternoon you come see me and Cuddles, Faye. You can play with him then. Maybe you could come every afternoon to play with him."

"Thank you! I'll ask my mom. I'm sure she'll let me." Faye patted Cuddles, then turned away. "See you tomorrow."

"I'll look forward to it."

Roxie walked with Faye into their yard, then looked back to see Barb Mayhew slip inside the back door with Cuddles in her arms. "Now we have to tell Mom and Dad."

Faye shrugged. "They'll understand. They know how it is with children and their need for a pet."

Roxie giggled. "Where'd you hear that?"

"On TV."

Roxie squeezed Faye's hand. "You're a great sister."

"I know." Faye giggled as she pressed her forehead against Roxie's arm.

A few minutes later Roxie led Faye into the kitchen where Mom and Dad sat at the table drinking steaming cups of tea. Faye pulled free and stopped in the middle of the room. She faced Mom and Dad with her head held high and her cheeks growing pink.

Roxie leaned against the island counter and watched. She knew how hard this was for Faye, but she was determined to help Faye set things right. Living with a guilty conscience is *hard*.

Faye took a deep breath and let it out.

"What's going on?" Dad asked.

"Faye?" Mom lifted an eyebrow questioningly as she set her cup down.

Faye flipped back her ponytails. "I did something wrong, and I came to confess and apologize."

Roxie saw the surprised looked on Mom's and Dad's faces. She felt very proud of Faye.

"I found a puppy in the backyard and sneaked him into the house and named him Cuddles and fed him peanut butter and jelly sandwiches." Faye told the entire story in almost one breath. "I'm sorry for disobeying and for everything else. Mrs. Mayhew says I can play with Cuddles every afternoon. That's what I'd like to do if you say I can."

Dad shook his head in amazement. "Well, well."

"So that's what I've been smelling," Mom said.

"Will you forgive me?" Faye looked ready to cry again.

"Yes," Mom and Dad said together as they hurried over to hug Faye.

Roxie smiled and slowly walked out of the kitchen. Too bad Lacy's and Eli's problems couldn't be solved this easily. Suddenly Roxie stopped. No problem was ever too big for God. Her eyes widened. God had dropped that thought into her head! And it was the truth! To her, some problems were big and others were little. To God, they were *all* little, *all* easy to solve! "But we have to let Him help us solve them," Roxie whispered in awe.

She ran to the phone and called Chelsea. When she answered, Roxie said, "Could I come over right now?"

"Sure. Kathy and Hannah are both here. We tried to call you to have you come over, but you weren't home then."

"See you in a couple of minutes." Roxie ran to get her jacket as she called, "I'm going to Chelsea's if you need me, Mom."

"Be back before 9," Dad called back.

"I will."

Before she opened the door, the phone rang. She ran to answer it in case it was Chelsea. It was Priscilla Adgate, and she sounded close to tears.

"Roxie, I wanted you to know how much I appreciate you girls praying for me. I'd like you to keep praying. I have a . . . problem to deal with, and I need God's help."

"We will pray for you." Roxie's stomach fluttered. "Is it about . . . your son Tad?"

"Yes! How did you know?"

"I heard something about him. My brother Eli's in school with him."

"Please *please* keep praying for him—and for me."

"We will."

"Thank you! And thank you again for the wonderful snow family and dog. And for the note."

"You're very welcome." Roxie smiled and hung up. She ran next door and right upstairs to Chelsea's bedroom. The Best Friends greeted her as if it had been days since they'd seen her and not just hours.

They sat in a circle on the floor, and Roxie told them about Mrs. Adgate's phone call, then about Eli and his secret meeting at midnight with Nate Irwin. It took a long time to tell because of all the comments the girls made. Roxie also told about Julie Pierson being scared about being home alone all the time and finally about Faye and Cuddles.

When she finished, Roxie sighed heavily and looked at the Best Friends. They were smiling at her as if they had a gigantic secret. "What?" she asked with a slight frown. "What?"

Chelsea, Kathy, and Hannah exchanged knowing looks. Finally Chelsea said, "I'll tell her."

Roxie's heart stopped, then raced alarmingly. "Tell me what?"

Smiling, Chelsea flipped back her bright red

hair. "We were praying for you—praying you'd tell us what was wrong—praying you'd know that God was always with you to help you."

"And God answered!" Kathy and Hannah cried excitedly.

Roxie laughed in delight as she tried to hug all the Best Friends at the same time.

When they settled down again, they prayed for Priscilla Adgate and then for Tad. Then they prayed for Eli, for Lacy, and for Roxie to know what to do to help them. Then they prayed for Julie Pierson and her parents. And they prayed for each other.

Later Roxie said, "I'm going to hide in the garage and listen to Eli and Nate. I will not let anyone persuade Eli to do something wrong!" She lifted her chin, and her eyes flashed. "I mean it!"

And she did mean it—with her whole heart. She loved Eli even if he did keep pushing her away. Somehow they'd be friends again.

11

Trouble

Trembling, Roxie tiptoed downstairs in the tiny light of the hall nightlight. Since she was going to hide in the garage, and the garage was cold, she was dressed in several layers of warm clothes, as much as if she were going sledding.

Roxie stopped at the bottom of the stairs and listened. The house was quiet because everyone was already in bed. Eli probably was waiting until almost midnight to go to the garage. Roxie wanted to be in a safe hiding-place before he went there.

In the garage she looked around for a hiding-place that would be safe and comfortable. The garage smelled like oil. The car and pickup stood side by side in the semidarkness. Could she hide in the back of the pickup? She shook her head. It would be terrible if Eli would decide to drive it somewhere with her stuck in the back. She wouldn't hide in the car either, for the same reason. She wasn't that brave!

Nervous chills raced up and down her spine as she frantically looked for the best hiding-place. Finally she settled on a place behind the riding lawn mower. She'd sit on the floor and be out of sight.

Just as she sat down, the door opened and Eli walked in, yawning. He didn't turn on the light. He wore a jacket but no cap or gloves. He coughed, then coughed again as he unlocked the side garage door that led outdoors. He opened it, and Roxie felt the blast of fresh, icy air. What if she suddenly sneezed? She bit back a horrified gasp.

Eli closed the door and looked out of the small windows in the top half of the door. He was silhouetted against the light from the streetlights.

The cold floor made Roxie shiver. Would Nate come on time? She hadn't realized how hard it would be to sit still in the cold garage without moving or making a sound.

Finally Eli opened the door again and said in a low voice, "Nate, I'm glad you could come. Tell me what to do now that Roxie gave me away."

Roxie's eyes widened in shock. What did he mean, gave him away?

Nate closed the door and leaned against it. He wore a heavy coat but no hat. "We'll have to get things going faster than we'd planned. Set up another meeting tomorrow night to discuss our next target."

Roxie's heart zoomed to her feet, and anguished tears filled her eyes. Eli was guilty! Her wonderful brother was a thief! She'd been so sure he wasn't—well, almost sure. Now, she'd made things worse for Eli by forcing him to do what Nate wanted him to do. Somehow she had to get Eli away from Nate and his dreadful plans. She had to stop him from breaking into another house.

"What if the boys won't let me go with them?" Eli sounded worried.

"They will. You're in tight with them since you stole the test for them. They'll believe anything you say."

Roxie covered her mouth to hold back a cry. Eli had stolen a test! What had happened to him? He'd been such a fine Christian boy for the past year. He must not have learned how to resist Satan when a temptation came. She remembered the Scripture, "Submit to God. Resist the Devil and he will flee from you." Eli hadn't submitted to God or resisted the Devil.

"I'll talk to them tomorrow, and then I'll call you when things are all set." Eli's voice trembled. "I hope this works, Nate."

"Me too! You keep that tracking device on you at all times. I want those boys."

Roxie frowned. What did Nate mean? Did he

want the boys to work for him? Wasn't he already a part of their gang? What was a tracking device? She'd heard about something like that on TV police shows, but she wasn't sure what Nate was talking about.

Nate and Eli talked a while longer. Nate finally left, and Eli closed and locked the door. He turned to go back inside when a sneeze exploded from near the pickup.

Roxie almost fell over. Who had sneezed?

Eli stopped short. "All right, Roxie. I know it's you. Come out where I can see you!"

But Roxie didn't move. She hadn't sneezed. But who had?

"Come on, Roxie! Don't play games!" Eli sounded really mad.

Roxie stayed right where she was. Her whole insides quivered. Who else was hiding in the garage?

Eli stepped toward the pickup. "Roxie, don't be dumb! Come here right now before I turn on the light. I know you're behind the pickup."

Roxie sank lower. She would not stand up even if he turned on the light. She had to know who was in the garage. Could it be Lacy? Or Faye?

Eli walked around the pickup without turning on the light. "Come on, Roxie. Why are you doing this?"

Barely breathing, Roxie bit the inside of her lower lip and waited.

Eli tapped the side of the pickup. "All right, stay hidden then! Just don't stay out here and freeze. And don't you dare tell anyone what you heard Nate and me say tonight."

Roxie waited in silence as Eli walked back into the house. Slowly she stood up. Blood roared in her ears. Who was hiding in the garage? She took a steadying breath. "Who . . . who's in here?"

Someone stood up in the back of the pickup. "It's me, Roxie . . . It's Julie."

"Julie!" Roxie gasped in shock, unable to believe what she was seeing.

Julie climbed out, huddling inside her jacket as she walked over to Roxie. "I'm freezing."

"What are you doing here?"

Julie shrugged. "I ran away from home," she said in a tiny voice.

"No!"

"I didn't know where else to go."

"I can't believe this."

"You're the only friend I have." Julie started to cry softly, then sobbed hard until she was shaking all over. "My only friend . . . The only one who cares."

Roxie slipped an arm around Julie and awkwardly patted her back. "We have to go inside where it's warm."

"I can't!"

"You have to!"

118

"I don't want my mom and dad to know where I am."

"Just come inside where it's warm."

Julie shivered. "I am cold—sooo cold!"

Roxie led Julie inside and locked the door behind them. Had Mom and Dad heard them come in? When no sound came from their bedroom down the hall, Roxie breathed easier. She held Julie's arm and walked upstairs with her. Roxie closed her bedroom door, turned on the light, and faced Julie. Her face was white and her eyes red-rimmed. "Why did you run away?"

Julie shrugged. "I tried to tell them I was afraid to be alone, but they wouldn't listen. They were busy getting ready to go to a movie." Julie couldn't go on for a while. "They told me to go to my room so I'd be out of the way." Julie sniffed and rubbed her hand across her nose. "I am always in the way!" She sank down on the chair in front of the desk. "After they left, I rode my bike here and hid in the garage."

"Oh, Julie! You've been out there for hours!"

"I know."

"Are you hungry?"

"I guess." Julie nodded. "Yes . . . Yes, I am."

"Let's go get you something to eat."

Julie's eyes widened in alarm. "Your folks will hear us."

"They'll understand." But would they? They

just had to! This was different from Faye sneaking in a puppy. Julie needed help desperately.

A few minutes later Roxie sat across the kitchen table from Julie while she ate a bowl of cornflakes with a sliced banana in it.

"Maybe we should call your folks," Roxie said in a low voice to keep from waking her mother and father.

Julie shook her head. "I'll never talk to them. I mean it, Roxie. They don't love me, so I've stopped loving them."

Roxie knew it wouldn't do any good to argue. Maybe after Julie got a good night's sleep she'd feel differently. That's what Mom always said anyway.

But the next morning Julie still refused to call her parents. Roxie loaned Julie some clean underwear, jeans, and a sweater to wear to school.

"Are you sure your mom won't see me?" Julie asked for the third time since she'd taken a shower.

"Trust me! Go out the front door and walk to the end of the street to catch the bus. I'll go out the back door like I always do and will meet you on the way." Roxie quickly made her bed as she tried to think of ways to get Julie to agree to call her folks.

Roxie dropped her big white teddy bear on her pillow and turned to Julie. "Please let me tell my mom about you. She'll know what to do. She'll want to help you."

"Will she make me go home?"

Roxie hesitated. She knew Mom. "She might."

"Then don't tell her!"

Roxie sighed heavily.

Julie clasped her hands together and looked pleadingly into Roxie's face. "Promise?"

Roxie frowned and finally nodded. "I promise." Was this going to get her in as much trouble as her promise to Eli? Maybe she should do what Mrs. Murphy had suggested—tell her folks because some promises weren't safe to keep. She wouldn't decide right now, but she would think about it.

A few minutes later the two girls crept downstairs. Julie slipped out the front door, and Roxie hurried to the kitchen.

Mom was just hanging up the phone. She turned to Roxie. "You won't believe this, but middle school is canceled again. The heat went out again during the night."

"Oh, no!" Roxie's heart dropped to her feet. She had to catch Julie before she got on the bus! "I've got to catch a friend of mine!"

"That's not necessary. Everybody here at The Ravines knows about the school closing."

Roxie ran to the closet and grabbed her jacket. She had to stop Julie!

"Roxie!" Mom called. "What's wrong?"

"I'll be right back, Mom!" Roxie ran outdoors and gasped as the cold air hit her. Boys and girls on their way to elementary school or high school walked along the sidewalks on both sides of the street. Roxie frantically looked for Julie's bright green and yellow jacket. Roxie raced down the sidewalk. Not a single green and yellow jacket was in sight.

Roxie stopped at the end of the sidewalk where the bus always stopped. Several kids were already waiting, but Julie wasn't there. Roxie frowned. Where was she?

12

Julie

Roxie stopped inside her garage and looked around. Julie's bike was gone, just as she'd suspected. Had Julie ridden home because she knew her parents would be gone, or was she on her way to the mall to hang out there for the day?

Slowly Roxie walked inside and pulled off her jacket. She smelled coffee and toast.

Mom was just leaving to take Faye to preschool. Mom kissed Roxie's cheek. "Grandma and I are going to Grand Rapids today. Would you like to go with us?"

"No. I'm going to see if the girls and I can bake cookies for Mrs. Murphy today instead of Thursday. I might go to the mall to see my friend Julie too."

"Just leave me a note. Be home for dinner."

"I will." Roxie walked slowly to the kitchen for breakfast. Nothing sounded good, but she ate a banana and drank a glass of milk anyway, so she wouldn't get hungry later. She set her glass in the dishwasher, sighed heavily, and called Julie.

Mrs. Pierson answered on the first ring. She sounded frantic.

Roxie almost hung up but thought she'd better say something. "Hi. May I speak to Julie?"

"Who's speaking?"

"Roxie Shoulders." She leaned weakly against the island counter. "Is Julie home?"

"No! I thought she might be with you. She told us all about you and three other girls—Chelsea, Hannah, and Kathy. She says the five of you are best friends."

Roxie tugged at the top of her sweater that suddenly felt too hot. How could she tell Mrs. Pierson the truth? But Roxie knew how she could—with strength from Jesus. Being truthful really was the best. "Mrs. Pierson, Julie and I met for the first time at the mall the other day. Before that we only knew each other by sight."

"But that's not true. Julie said you were best friends."

"Julie didn't want you to know that she doesn't have any friends. She spends all her free time at the mall."

"At the mall?" Mrs. Pierson sounded very upset.

"She's afraid to be home alone because of all

the break-ins in the neighborhood. And she's always lonely."

A sob broke from Mrs. Pierson. "Where is she now?"

"I don't know. Probably at the mall."

"It's not even open yet!"

"The doors are unlocked for people who want to walk for exercise."

"Oh." Mrs. Pierson was quiet a long time. "Where did she spend the night?"

"With me. But I didn't find her until late. She was hiding in our garage because she didn't want to be home alone."

Another sob broke from Mrs. Pierson. "Why didn't she tell me?"

"I think you should ask her when you find her."

"She might not say. Please, tell me."

Roxie twisted the phone cord around and around her finger. "Are you sure you want to hear this?"

"Yes!"

Roxie swallowed hard. "She doesn't think you like her."

"What?" Mrs. Pierson's voice rose. "What do you mean?"

Roxie wanted to hang up, but she forced herself to continue. "She says you and her dad are always busy with each other—working, going out for dessert, going to the movies, and so on. She says she's always in the way."

"But we only wanted to give her her own space."

Roxie frowned. She'd never heard a mom talk that way in her life. Parents were known to butt in where they didn't belong—that's the way it was supposed to be. "Julie said she'd rather have attention from you."

"But we see that all her needs are met. She dresses very well for a girl her age." Her voice broke. "When she's sixteen we plan to buy her her own car. We've told her that."

Roxie rolled her eyes. Her own car! Not even Eli had his own car. But then she knew what she needed to say to Mrs. Pierson at that very moment. "Julie would rather have your love."

Mrs. Pierson cried softly into the phone. "I didn't realize . . ."

"I was going to go to the mall to look for her."

"I'll go. I've already called to say I won't be at work. I'll call my husband to tell him everything."

"Julie will be glad to see you even if she doesn't act like it. Be patient with her." Roxie bit back a laugh. She sounded like her mother.

"Thank you, Roxie." Mrs. Pierson was quiet a while. "Are your parents Burt and Ilene Shoulders?"

"Yes."

"And you live at The Ravines?"

"Yes."

"After I find Julie and we talk, we'd like to come see you and your parents. Could we do that?"

"I guess. My mom will probably be home by 4. You could call her then."

"I will. And, Roxie, thanks."

"You're welcome. Will you call me if you don't find Julie?"

"Yes."

Roxie said good-bye and hung up. She had to call the Best Friends so they could pray for Julie. Before Roxie could pick up the receiver, the phone rang. She scooped it up and said, "Hello."

"Hi, Roxie. Can you come over right now? Hannah and Kathy will be here soon."

"Sure." Roxie hung up, grabbed her jacket, and ran next door to Chelsea's. The sun was out and was warm enough to melt the snow. The tunnel to the igloo across the street had a hole melted through it. Soon the igloo would just be a pile of snow. That made Roxie feel sad. She wanted the igloo to last the rest of the winter.

In Chelsea's bedroom Roxie sat on the desk and listened to Chelsea tell about a phone conversation with Brody.

"I'm thinking about taking guitar lessons." Her eyes sparkling, Chelsea sat cross-legged in the middle of her bed. Her red hair hung down on her yellow sweater. She was wearing her newest jeans.

Chelsea had enough clothes for five girls. "Don't you think that would be fun?"

Roxie grinned. "Especially if Brody gave you lessons."

"Exactly!" Chelsea giggled.

Just then Hannah and Kathy walked in, bringing in a smell of fresh, cold air. They said hello and sat on the bed.

Chelsea smiled at the girls. "I called Mrs. Murphy a while ago, and she said we could bake cookies today if we wanted instead of Thursday after school. I vote we go. Who votes yes?"

The girls raised their hands and giggled. Chelsea always wanted the meetings to be proper meetings.

"Good." Chelsea nodded. "Nobody votes no. Any other business before we go?"

Roxie held up her hand as high as her chin.

Chelsea raised her red brows. "Yes, Roxie?"

"I'd like us to pray for Julie Pierson." Roxie quickly told the story. "So, can we pray now?"

"Yes." Chelsea looked very solemn as she scooted off the bed and onto her knees. The girls held hands, and Hannah prayed for Julie and her parents.

■

At the mall Julie listlessly walked out of the restroom and along the quiet walkway between the closed stores. She looked in windows without seeing the displays. She should've gone to the bus and to school, but once she'd left Roxie's house, she just couldn't do it. She had to be alone for a while to try to sort out her life. What would she do with herself? She couldn't stay at Roxie's forever.

Her stomach grumbled with hunger. Maybe she should get something to eat. But she didn't feel like eating. She felt like curling up in a ball and crying until she didn't have any tears left.

She stopped at a toy store and looked unseeingly in the window. Did Mom and Dad even know she was gone? Had they checked on her last night or this morning? Probably not. Why should they? They'd expect her to be there—on the fringes of their lives where she didn't count.

Tears stung her eyes, and she blinked them away. Maybe she should tell them how she felt. She sighed heavily. What good would that do?

Slowly she walked on, her head down and her shoulders bent. She'd love to have parents like Roxie's, even though they seemed really strict at times from what Roxie had said.

Julie looked longing toward Beverly's, wishing it was open so she could try on clothes, forget about her heartache, and think only about shopping.

Just then someone touched her arm. She bit back a shriek as she turned her head. Her eyes widened in shock. She'd halfway expected to see Roxie, but instead it was her mom. Her blonde hair was cut short to make her look younger. She wore dark pink lipstick that matched her blouse.

"Hi, Julie," Claire Pierson said softly.

"Mom!" Julie didn't know if she should cry or run away.

"Roxie was looking for you. She called the house."

"Did she call from school?"

Claire shook her head. "Middle school was canceled again today. Roxie was worried about you." Claire dabbed a tear from her eye. "So was I."

Julie didn't believe that for a second. "I'm just fine, as you can see. You go to work, and I'll shop."

"Let's go have breakfast and talk instead." Claire managed to smile. "Roxie said you didn't eat this morning."

"Roxie talks too much!"

"She's a very good friend, in my opinion." Claire slipped a hand through Julie's arm and walked to Elias Brothers, a cheerful restaurant that was already open for breakfast customers. Claire asked for a booth in the back of the room, then ordered French toast and milk for Julie and coffee and a roll for herself.

Julie sat nervously on her icy hands. Was she dreaming? Mom didn't do this kind of thing with her. Mom's diamond studs flashed in her ears as she moved her head. The tangy perfume she always wore wafted across the table. It wasn't a dream.

Mom was real. "Why aren't you at work?" Julie asked sharply. Her voice sounded loud in the quiet restaurant.

Claire took a deep breath. "Your dad and I were alarmed when you weren't in bed last night when we returned. We searched for a note but couldn't find one. So I stayed awake, expecting a call." She blinked away tears. "We thought about calling the police, but we didn't want to embarrass you, so we didn't call them."

Julie could barely believe what she was hearing. Was it possible Mom and Dad cared about her after all?

"This morning I was frantic. We called the hospitals to see if you'd been hurt and taken in, but of course you weren't there. Then Roxie called." Claire cleared her throat and dabbed carefully at her eyes. "I was relieved, to say the least. So was your dad."

Her head spinning, Julie sipped her ice water. It soothed her dry throat.

"Roxie told me how you've been feeling."

Julie's eyes widened in alarm. "How could she do that to me? I told her in confidence!"

"I begged her to tell me, so we could settle this immediately." Claire's eyes filled with tears again. "Julie, we love you. But we didn't want to suffocate you. We didn't want to bore you with our wants and expectations. We wanted you to have the freedom for friends and activities. But we were wrong. You needed our love and attention. We didn't realize that." Tears slipped down Claire's cheeks. "We thought by giving you your own space, we were loving you. Please, please forgive us, and please accept how imperfect we are."

Julie's heart stood still. For sure this was a dream. Oh, but she didn't want to wake up and find an empty seat across from her!

Just then the waitress brought the food. Steam rose from the French toast as butter melted across the top of the pieces. "If you need anything else, please let me know." The waitress smiled. "Have a good breakfast." She walked away to wait on someone else.

Julie touched the French toast. It was real! She looked across at Mom sipping her coffee. She was still there. She was real too! Roxie had said she'd prayed for her. Had this miracle happened as an answer to Roxie's prayers?

Finally Julie smiled and poured syrup over her French toast. "Mom, thanks for coming after me," she said softly.

"You're very welcome."

Just then Ron Pierson stopped at the table. "Is there food enough for me?"

Julie gasped in surprise. "I thought you were at work, Dad."

"I was, but I wanted to see you—to make sure you were all right." He pulled off his overcoat and sat beside Claire. "I thought I'd come have breakfast with the two of you."

Claire smiled. "We're glad."

"Very glad." Julie wanted to say more, but the words stuck in her throat. She'd find a way to say everything later.

■

At Mrs. Murphy's house the Best Friends stood at the island counter with Kesha and mixed the cookie dough. They talked and laughed and tried not to make any mistakes as they measured the ingredients. Mrs. Murphy sat at the kitchen table with a cup of herbal tea and a bran muffin.

Chelsea popped a few chocolate chips into her mouth and chewed them. She liked the bittersweet taste of the chocolate.

Roxie thought about Julie. If she was at the mall, her mom had probably found her. Would they settle everything by talking? She'd call Julie at home later to see.

Kesha stopped stirring her batch of chocolate chocolate-chip cookies and looked at the girls. "I heard that Priscilla Adgate went to the high school to get her son Tad yesterday. He wouldn't talk to her, and she ran away in tears."

Roxie gripped the wooden spoon tightly. "That's terrible!" Had she found out Tad was suspected of the break-ins?

"We could go see her again," Hannah said

softly. "We could see if she wants us to do something for her."

Kathy nodded. "Let's do!"

Mrs. Murphy looked up from her tea. "Take her some cookies when they're baked."

Roxie smiled. "That could be our good deed." And they'd pray for Mrs. Adgate too, just as they had before.

13

Secrets Revealed

Roxie held the paper plate of cookies covered with plastic wrap while Chelsea rang Priscilla Adgate's front doorbell. Hannah and Kathy were admiring the snow family. The sun had melted an ear off the dog, but Roxie planned to fix it before they went home.

Priscilla opened the door. The heat from the house drifted out around her. "Girls! What a nice surprise!"

Smiling, Roxie held out the cookies. "We brought these for you."

"That's very sweet of you." With a wide smile Priscilla took the plate and stepped aside. "Come in for a while, can you?"

The Best Friends looked at each other, then nodded and smiled. Roxie stepped in first. The house was hot and smelled like cinnamon. She slipped off her jacket so she wouldn't melt down into her sneakers. She noticed the others were doing the same. Chelsea probably liked the extra heat since she was from Oklahoma where winters weren't as cold as in Michigan.

Priscilla led the girls to the kitchen. The sun shone through the row of windows in back of the round maple table. She set the plate of cookies on the table beside a basket of wooden green apples. "Will you girls have cookies and milk with me?"

Roxie's stomach turned over at the thought of more cookies, and she forced back a groan. She'd eaten cookies and cookie dough until she couldn't stand another bite. She knew the others felt the same way. She rested her hand on the tall back of the maple chair. "Thanks for the offer, but we couldn't eat one more cookie right now. We've been baking cookies all morning."

Nodding, Priscilla laughed. "I understand. Could we sit down anyway? I want to ask you something."

The girls sat at the table with Priscilla Adgate. Roxie locked her hands in her lap. Was Mrs. Adgate going to ask about Tad? It would be very hard to tell her that her son could possibly have been in on the break-ins.

Priscilla leaned forward slightly. "I want you girls to know what a great blessing you've been to me."

The girls looked at each other in surprise. They

hadn't done anything special. All they'd done was build the snow family, pray for her, and bring her a plate of cookies.

Priscilla brushed at a tear. "I had forgotten God loved me and my family." She flushed. "I had forgotten how much God meant to me. Your kindness and your prayers and the Scripture you wrote in your note reminded me of how far I'd strayed from God."

Roxie swelled with pride. It felt good to know they'd encouraged Mrs. Adgate that much.

Hannah smiled. "We're glad we could help."

Chelsea and Kathy nodded.

Careful not to smear her eye makeup, Priscilla dabbed away her tears with a white paper napkin. "I was ready to give up on my son, but you reminded me that God answers prayer. I won't give up on him! I'll pray for him until I get him back. Would you girls pray for him too?"

Roxie froze, but the others nodded. Did they remember that Mrs. Adgate's son was Tad Woodley? And Tad was probably one of the thieves Eli was involved with.

Several minutes later the girls left the house, and Roxie breathed a sigh of relief. Could she pray for Tad when all she wanted to do was see him go to jail and away from Eli?

Later the girls walked into Chelsea's house and

up to her bedroom. Chelsea touched Roxie. "What's wrong?"

Roxie pulled away and sat at the desk. "What makes you think something is?"

"We can tell," Hannah said as she sat cross-legged on the floor with her back against Chelsea's bed.

Roxie rubbed her finger back and forth on her watchband. Why try to keep her thoughts to herself? The Best Friends always found out *everything* about each other. That's how best friends are.

With a catch in her voice Roxie told the girls how she felt about Tad and why. She told about Nate's visit to Eli and all they'd said. "So, how can I pray for Tad when I'm so mad at him?"

Kathy patted Roxie's leg. "I know how, and so do you. You first forgive Tad and Eli, and then you pray for both of them."

Roxie sucked in her breath. Forgive? How could she? But she already knew the answer—she could forgive with Jesus' help.

"We're here with you," Hannah said softly.

"I know." Roxie's eyes blurred with tears. "I'm glad too."

They bowed their heads and prayed together for Roxie, and then Roxie forgave Tad and Eli. She prayed for Tad and for his mother. Her voice quivering, she prayed for Eli too.

Later the girls sat quietly a while—Hannah and

Kathy on the floor, Chelsea on her bed, and Roxie on the chair at the desk. Finally Hannah jumped up, her eyes wide. "Did you say Nate Irwin gave Eli something called a tracking device?"

Roxie nodded. "Why?"

"If Nate is in with the gang of thieves, why would he need a tracking device to learn where they were meeting?"

"That's right!" Kathy nodded, and Chelsea agreed.

"So what are you saying?" Roxie frowned thoughtfully while a little ray of hope sparked inside her.

"You told us Julie Pierson thought Nate was a cop." Hannah looked ready to explode with excitement. "What if he is?"

Roxie gasped.

Chelsea's eyes sparkled. "If Nate is a cop, and if Eli is working with Nate, that means Eli is helping the police!"

Roxie shivered again and again. "Is it possible?"

"I'd sure rather believe Eli is helping the police than what we've been thinking," Hannah said crisply. She'd loved Eli a long time, and she didn't want to think he'd do anything really bad.

Her face ashen, Roxie clutched her throat. "I hope I didn't put Eli in danger by spying on him! He said I ruined everything."

"We'll have to do what we can to help," Kathy said.

Hannah nodded. "We'll think of something."

Roxie swallowed hard. "It might be smarter to stay out of the way. I don't want to do *anything* to hurt Eli."

■

His nerves tight, Eli waited at Tad Woodley's locker. Noisy students hurried along the hall to catch their bus. Other students clanged locker doors shut. The smell of wet wool and cigarette smoke filled the area. Eli watched for Tad, and he finally saw him coming. Tad stopped at the locker for his jacket. He had a medium build, brown hair that needed to be cut, and blue eyes. Eli forced a smile. "Am I included in the meeting tonight?"

Tad barely nodded. "Gabe and Wayne will be there too."

"I don't understand why we can't know where we go for the meetings." Eli kept his voice from breaking in fear.

Scowling, Tad slipped on his faded denim jacket. "The man who takes what we steal doesn't want us to know his identity."

"I realize that. But why doesn't he?"

"So that if we get caught, we can't turn him in."

Eli frowned. "That doesn't seem fair to us. Why should we pay for it and him get off free?"

Tad jabbed Eli's arm. "You want out?"

"No!"

"Then don't ask so many dumb questions." Tad walked toward the door with Eli beside him. "We're minors, so if we get caught, we won't get sent to prison. Bear would."

Eli's pulse quickened. Bear! No one had called the man by name before. But what good would knowing just *Bear* be to Nate? Eli wanted to ask more about the man called Bear, but he bit back the questions. He'd been blindfolded when he went to the meetings to learn how to slip inside a house, rob it, and slip back out in record time. The meetings were held in the early evenings so that parents of the high school students wouldn't question them. He'd gone to two meetings already. The man called Bear, their "teacher," wore a mask over his eyes. He was tall and, dressed in a fuzzy brown sweater, looked like a bear. Eli hadn't been able to tell Nate who the man was or where he lived. After tonight Nate would know. The tracking device would lead Nate right to Bear.

Eli lifted his hand in a half-wave. "See you tonight."

Tad nodded without smiling. "At 8."

Eli hurried outdoors to the bus and sat toward the back. He had to calm himself down before he got home. Mom sometimes looked at him as if she were reading his mind. That would never do. He couldn't tell his parents what was going on until it was over. He'd promised Nate.

Eli leaned his head back and closed his eyes. The familiar smells and noise of the students in the bus drifted around him, soothing him a little. It was exciting but nerve-racking to work for Nate. After this maybe Eli would know if he wanted to be a policeman after he graduated from high school. It was hard to know what he wanted to do with his life. Dad had said to pray about it. He had, but so far he hadn't heard an answer.

Someone laughed with a laugh that sounded like Roxie's. Eli sighed heavily. He shouldn't have yelled at her for trying to help him. Would she forgive him after she learned what he'd really been up to?

■

Her heart heavy, Lacy stuck her purse on the shelf and hung her jacket on the rack reserved for Markee's employees. She flipped back her long auburn hair and pulled her yellow and white sweater down over her yellow slacks. She turned and almost bumped into Peggy Brown, a high school girl who worked in the same department. Lacy backed away. More than anything she wanted to get away from Peggy!

"What's wrong?" Peggy laid her purse on the shelf and hung up her jacket. "Is it Mrs. Turner again?"

Lacy frowned. Why would Peggy say that? Peggy was the one causing all the trouble, not Mrs. Turner. "What do you mean?"

Peggy fingered the necklace resting on her green blouse. "I really don't want to tell you this, but Mrs. Turner has it in for you. I think she's trying to make you quit your job."

"What?" Lacy felt weak all over. Was it possible? "But why?"

Peggy shrugged. "I have no idea. Maybe she doesn't think you make enough sales."

"But I make more than you!"

"I know." Peggy shrugged. "I can't figure it out." She pinned on her name tag. "I shouldn't tell you this, but I decided it was only fair . . . Mrs. Turner told me she saw you steal something."

Lacy's eyes widened in shock. "I never did! Why would Mrs. Turner say such a thing? She has always been nice to me!"

"Sure, she is—behind your back." Peggy wagged her finger at Lacy. "If I were you, I'd ask Mrs. Turner why she's lying about you."

"Maybe I will!" Her hands trembling, Lacy pinned on her name tag. Maybe she'd talk to Mrs. Turner before she went on duty! But did she have the nerve? She didn't want to lose her job.

■

With the receiver held to her ear, Roxie leaned against the wall outside Lacy's bedroom and waited for Julie to come to the phone. Her mother had answered and said Julie would be right there. Roxie had tried to call Julie four times already, but she hadn't gotten an answer until just now. Smells of dinner drifted upstairs along with Faye's laughter. What was taking Julie so long to come to the phone? Roxie's nerves stretched tight.

"Hi, Roxie."

"Hi, Julie! How'd it go with your folks?"

Julie laughed and actually sounded happy! "We talked, Roxie. For the first time in years! It was wonderful!"

Roxie sagged weakly against the wall. "I'm glad."

"Yeah, me too. They love me, Roxie. They do!"

"Oh, Julie, aren't you glad you finally told them how you feel?"

"Yes. It's all because of you, Roxie. Thank you!"

Julie's thanks wrapped around Roxie's heart and brought a smile to her face. "So, do you think you'll still be afraid to stay hcme alone?"

Julie sighed. "Yes. I wish I wouldn't be, but I am. Especially when Nate Irwin is a thief instead of a cop like I thought."

Roxie gripped the receiver until her knuckles turned white. Should she tell Julie that Nate was probably a cop after all? But if she told Julie, maybe it would get out and mess up Eli's plans. Roxie's head whirled. She knew she had to keep quiet about Nate and Eli. "If you're ever afraid when you're alone, call me and we'll talk."

"Thanks. And, Roxie, thanks for being a friend."

Roxie chuckled. "We had fun at the mall, didn't we?"

"Sure did."

Roxie twisted the cord around her finger. "I should tell you why I was there so much."

"Yes. Tell me!"

Roxie took a deep breath. "I was having big problems at home that I didn't know how to settle. But I've learned that praying is better than going crazy at the mall. I think praying is the answer for you too."

"You're right, Roxie."

"Why don't you come to church with me Sunday? We have a great class for our age group. You'll know a lot of the kids there from school."

"Sounds good."

"We have an assignment to write about our families. I guess it's to help us get to know them better."

"I like that."

"So, will you come?"

"I'll see what my folks say." Julie giggled. "That was really nice to say. Before today I would've made my plans without considering them. It's soooo wonderful to have parents who care about me!"

"I know." Roxie thought about the time she'd been embarrassed because her dad wore paint-stained, ragged overalls in public—right out where people could see him. Finally she'd learned to love him even if he wore clothes she wished he didn't. Love doesn't care about paint-stained, ragged overalls!

Roxie and Julie talked a while longer, and then Roxie said good-bye and hung up. She knew Eli was in his bedroom, but she didn't have the courage to talk to him. She didn't want him yelling at her again. It hurt too much.

Just then Lacy ran up the stairs and hurried to her room. She was crying hard.

Roxie caught Lacy's bedroom door before she slammed it shut and entered her sister's room. "Lacy, what's wrong?"

Lacy helplessly shook her head. "Get out of here," she said between sobs.

"I want to help you!"

"How?" Lacy's eyes flashed with anger. "By making Mrs. Turner stop telling lies about me? By making her keep me on at Markee's?"

Roxie slowly closed Lacy's door. "I thought Peggy Brown was the one causing trouble for you."

"So did I!" Lacy flopped down on her chair and

kicked off her shoes. "But I was wrong! It was Mrs. Turner all along."

"How do you know?"

Lacy's cheeks reddened. "Because Peggy said so! She told me what Mrs. Turner said about me— that I stole from the store, checked in late all the time, was rude to customers!"

Frowning, Roxie sank to the edge of Lacy's wide bed. "Lacy, I heard Peggy talking to Mrs. Turner about you."

Lacy sat still with her hands locked in her lap. "What did you hear?" she whispered hoarsely.

"All the things you said Mrs. Turner said. Only it was Peggy who said them to Mrs. Turner."

Lacy frowned. "Are you sure?"

"Very sure. Mrs. Turner told Peggy to keep her thoughts to herself."

"She did?"

"Mrs. Turner didn't seem to like hearing bad things about you from Peggy."

"This is unbelievable!" Lacy brushed tears off her cheeks. "Roxie, you aren't just saying this to make me feel better, are you?"

Roxie shook her head. "I honestly heard Peggy say those things."

"Why would she want me to quit working at Markee's?"

"Who knows. Maybe so she can get more hours for herself."

147

Lacy jumped up. "Or maybe because I saw her shoplifting and she's afraid I'll tell!"

"Did you see her stealing?"

"Yes! But I said I wouldn't tell as long as she didn't do it again. She promised she wouldn't."

"But she doesn't trust you to keep quiet."

"Right!" Lacy pulled Roxie up and hugged her hard. "Thank you, Roxie! You saved my life!"

Roxie's eyes filled with sudden tears. Lacy hadn't shoved her aside, and Lacy had actually thanked her for helping her! "So what'll you do now?"

"Go right back to work! I left early because I wasn't feeling well. I wasn't feeling well because of what Peggy had said. Now I'll settle the problem!" Lacy looked determined. For the first time in a long time her eyes sparkled.

"Want me to go with you?"

Lacy shook her head, then laughed and squeezed Roxie's hand. "Sure—why not? We'll take care of this problem together."

Roxie's face lit up. Together! She and Lacy were going to do something together! When God answered prayer, He did a fantastic job of it!

14

Eli's Adventure

Butterflies fluttered in Roxie's stomach as she got off the escalator right behind Lacy. Music floated around her along with the sweet aroma of perfume. Shoppers hurried past, talking and laughing.

Her face pale, Lacy stopped at the teen department where she worked and turned to Roxie. "Are you very sure about Peggy Brown?"

"Positive!" Roxie trembled. What if she'd misunderstood? Things like that happened. No! She hadn't misunderstood! "God is with you, Lacy."

Lacy lifted her chin and looked determined. "That's right!"

Just then Roxie spotted Peggy talking to an eighth-grade girl near the T-shirts. Roxie nudged Lacy and whispered, "Peggy's over there."

"I see her. And Mrs. Turner is near the cash register. She's alone." Lacy took a step forward, then stopped. "This is really *really* hard."

"But you can do it!"

"Yes—yes, I can!" Lacy's cheeks turned bright red as she hurried down the aisle to Mrs. Turner.

She spotted Lacy and smiled. "You're back."

"Yes. I had to come back to talk to you." Lacy pulled Roxie to her side. "This is my sister Roxie."

Mrs. Turner smiled but had a questioning look in her eye. "Hello, Roxie."

"Hi." Roxie's mouth was dry.

Lacy took a deep breath. "Mrs. Turner, I went home because I was really upset."

"What about, Lacy?" Mrs. Turner sounded very concerned.

"About losing my job. I never stole anything from the store. And I'm never rude to customers."

"I know that." Mrs. Turner glanced toward Peggy, then back at Lacy. "You're a good worker."

"Thank you. So, you aren't considering letting me go?"

Roxie held her breath.

Mrs. Turner shook her head. "No, I'm definitely not."

Just then Roxie saw the customer walk away from Peggy. Roxie nudged Lacy. "We could talk to Peggy before another customer comes in."

"Good idea." Lacy faced Mrs. Turner squarely. "Would you talk to Peggy with me and get this whole thing settled?"

"I'd be glad to."

Roxie smiled with pride as she walked behind Lacy and Mrs. Turner and on over to Peggy. Roxie couldn't wait to tell the Best Friends every detail.

"Peggy, we want to speak to you," Lacy said, blocking Peggy's exit.

Peggy flushed scarlet. "I'm really too busy right now."

"You can take time for this," Mrs. Turner said firmly.

The color drained from Peggy's face. "Have I done something wrong?"

Lacy nodded. "You've lied about me to Mrs. Turner, and I want it stopped!"

Roxie almost burst with pride as Lacy told Peggy she knew what she'd been doing. Peggy tried to deny it, but she couldn't with Mrs. Turner standing right there.

Peggy burst into tears as she turned to Mrs. Turner. "What'll you do now?"

"If Lacy wants you fired, I'll fire you."

Roxie saw the struggle Lacy was having. Roxie knew it would be sooo easy to hold a grudge against Peggy and to say, "Fire her."

Lacy lifted her chin. "I don't want her fired, but I do want her to stop lying about me."

"I will. Honest." Peggy sounded desperate. "And I'll work harder. I need this job."

Mrs. Turner studied Peggy for a long time. Finally she nodded. "You may continue to work here at Markee's, but it'll be for a probationary period. I'll be watching you closely."

"I'll do my best! I promise!"

"Fine. Go back to work now." Mrs. Turner turned to Lacy. "Suppose you go to work too."

"I will. I'll drive Roxie home first and will be right back."

Roxie's heart leaped. Lacy wasn't going to make her walk home as she usually would have!

In the car Lacy smiled at Roxie. "Thanks for helping me."

Roxie smiled happily. "Anytime, Lacy. What are sisters for?"

■

With shivers slithering down his spine, Eli walked into the warmth of the house where the meeting was to be held. Finally he was allowed to take off the blindfold and his jacket. He put his glasses back on. Tad, Wayne, and Gabe, standing beside him, were taking off their blindfolds and jackets too. None of them looked happy, and none of them said anything. Eli suddenly wanted to leave. The tiny tracking device in his sock felt bigger than his fist and seemed to weigh more than Wayne Sinclair who weighed over two hundred pounds. Would Bear notice the tracking device?

Tad jabbed Eli and whispered, "Relax."

Eli sat on the folding chair beside Tad just as Bear walked into the room. Tonight he wore a blue sweater instead of the brown one he'd worn the other times. His black mask covered his eyes. Eli studied him through dark lashes. If he saw Bear on the street, would he recognize him? Could a mask really hide his identity that much?

With his hands on his hips, Bear stood in front of the boys. "We're going to do three more jobs here in Middle Lake, and then I'm moving on. It's important not to stay too long and give the cops a chance to get somebody on the inside."

Eli's skin prickled with fear. Was Bear looking at him? Did Bear know he was working undercover? Silently Eli prayed for God's protection and help.

Bear walked back and forth in front of the boys. The smell of coffee drifted from the kitchen. Bear stopped and glowered at the boys. "I want you each to do the job you're been assigned and then get back to the van. Never take it on yourself to take over a different job unless you see another guy is in trouble. We've been successful because we go in quick and get out quick."

Eli listened to Bear with one ear and to sounds outside the room with the other. Why didn't Nate burst in and arrest Bear and the boys?

Finally the meeting was over. Once again Eli tied on his blindfold. He wanted to tie it so he could peek under it, but he didn't dare. He walked to the van in the garage and sat inside. It smelled dusty and closed in.

The driver backed the van out of the garage. Eli frowned. He had no idea what part of town he was in, nor did he know the driver. Nobody talked as the driver stopped outside the mall. Eli pulled off his blindfold and put his glasses back on. He did as he was told and walked away from the van without looking back. The boys didn't talk but split up immediately. His heart racing, Eli hurried home. Cold wind blew against him as he walked. He wanted to yell in anger and frustration at the top of his lungs. He'd gone to the meeting with the tracking device, and nothing had happened! Had Nate lied to him?

At home Eli slipped in quietly so he wouldn't have to answer questions. He turned on his desk lamp and took out the tracking device. He laid it in his drawer, then sat with his head in his hands. He was home safely, but that didn't seem to be enough. He wanted things to turn out the way he'd planned.

Roxie had been waiting for Eli. She had been sure he would run into the house and shout his victory. But he hadn't. Had something dreadful happened?

Her heart thundering, Roxie knocked softly on Eli's door. Faye was already asleep for the night. Lacy wasn't home yet. Roxie waited, then knocked again. "Eli, it's me."

"Go away," Eli said tiredly.

Roxie started to turn away, then set her jaw

stubbornly and opened the door. Eli sat at his desk looking dejected. Tears pricked her eyes. She wanted to touch him, but she kept her hands at her sides. "Did something go wrong?"

He didn't look up. "Please get out of here, Roxie."

She took a step forward. "I want to help. I'm really sorry for making trouble for you."

Eli sighed heavily. "Come in and shut the door."

Roxie closed the door and sat on the edge of his bed. "Where's the tracking device?"

"So it was you in the garage!"

Roxie flushed. "I was there, but so was my friend Julie. She's the one who sneezed."

Eli shook his head. "I hope you didn't tell anyone what you heard."

Roxie took a deep breath. "I told Chelsea, Hannah, and Kathy. But they won't tell anyone. Honest!"

Eli rubbed a hand across his face and pushed up his glasses. "Roxie, Roxie . . ."

"We prayed for you."

He smiled before he knew he was going to.

She sighed in relief. "You're not mad at me anymore, are you?"

"I suppose not."

"Will you tell me what happened tonight?"

Eli leaned back in his chair. "I thought for sure

Nate would arrest them all tonight, but he didn't even show up." Eli told Roxie everything that had happened.

She frowned thoughtfully. "I saw a man, Mr. Blessman, who lives near Julie Pierson. *He* reminded me of a big bear. Do you think he could be Bear?"

"I don't know." Eli jumped up and paced his room. "I wish I knew what happened to Nate!"

"You did what you were supposed to do, Eli."

"It wasn't enough if the guys aren't stopped."

Just then the phone rang. Roxie and Eli both dashed down the hall to answer it. Eli reached it first and grabbed it eagerly. "Hello," he said in a strained voice. He held the phone so Roxie could hear too.

"Eli, it's Nate. We got 'em."

"Great! Who are they?"

"Carl Blessman and Jim Woodley."

Roxie almost fell over. She'd showed Mr. Blessman the pictures to have him identify the thieves, and he'd been the mastermind himself! Along with Tad's dad! "Ask about Tad," she whispered.

"What about the boys? What about Tad?"

"They're at the jail. We called their parents. Except for Tad's. He has only his dad, he says."

Roxie's eyes widened, and she shook her head. "He has a mom—Priscilla Adgate."

"Tad has a mom," Eli said. "Priscilla Adgate." He read off her phone number as Roxie wrote it down on a pad next to the phone.

"Tad's mad at his mom," Roxie whispered.

Eli repeated the message.

"But she wants to help him. She loves him."

Again Eli repeated the message. "Why didn't you come in while we were there?"

Nate chuckled. "We knew there was someone else—another adult. I held the officers back for several minutes. Jim Woodley came out with Blessman, laughing and talking and making plans. We heard them and arrested them. They were very surprised."

Roxie smiled. It was all taken care of. She could call Julie and tell her everything was all right. Julie would really be surprised about Mr. Blessman.

Finally Eli hung up. "They got 'em!"

"I can't believe it!"

Eli hugged Roxie close and let out a loud whoop.

Roxie laughed. "Shhh. You'll wake up Faye."

Eli ran down the hall. "I'm going to tell Mom and Dad. Now they can stop worrying about me!"

Roxie ran right behind him to the living room. She listened as he told Mom and Dad everything. They were astonished, and even angry at times because of the danger he'd been in, but finally their anger turned to pride. Roxie sat in the corner of the couch and smiled so hard, her face hurt.

"I guess this teaches me we should trust you no matter how things look," Mom said, kissing Eli.

Roxie's eyes widened. Trust! That's what she'd write about for Sunday school—how important it was to trust God, trust her family, and trust her friends. All her heartache had come about because she hadn't trusted. Hopefully after this she'd remember to trust.

Just then Lacy ran into the living room. Her face glowed, and she was laughing. "Mom, Dad, wait'll you hear!" Lacy turned to Roxie. "Did you tell them?"

"No. I thought you'd want to."

"Tell us what?"

Lacy flung her arms wide. "I talked to Mrs. Turner. She doesn't want me to leave! She likes my work, and she likes me!"

Laughing, Roxie listened as Lacy told Mom and Dad what had been bothering her for the past several weeks.

"I can't believe what's happened to you and to Eli," Mom said with tears in her eyes.

Dad shook his head as he slowly stood up and walked from his chair to the fireplace and then to the door. He looked at Lacy on the arm of the couch, Eli on the floor, and Roxie in the corner of the couch. "Kids, I don't ever want this to happen again. Your mom and I are your parents. We're here to help you with everything."

Mom nodded. "We want you to talk to us."

Dad folded his arms across his chest. "We haven't been a Christian family for very long, but we're one now. That means we live by different rules than before. We talk about our problems, and then we pray about them. Jesus is the head of this house. We can trust Him to help us solve everything."

Roxie hadn't heard Dad talk like this before. The Best Friends had told her their dads always did, but this was a first for the Shoulders family. Roxie smiled. It felt good to have a dad who wanted to help them do what Jesus wanted.

Just then Faye ran into the room, a teddy bear under her arm. She was flushed, and her hair was flying around her head. She looked around at everyone with a frown. "Is this a family meeting? Did you vote for us to get a dog?"

Roxie laughed with the others as Dad picked Faye up and hugged her tight.

Roxie glanced at her watch. It was too late to call the Best Friends and tell them all that had happened. She'd see them in the morning on the bus if the furnace at the middle school was working again, and she'd tell them *everything*.

She smiled. They'd be as happy as she was to hear the outcome for Lacy and for Eli. The Best Friends would want to hear every word. That's what Best Friends were like.

Roxie knew that no matter what happened to her and to the Best Friends and to their families and friends, Jesus would always be their very Best Friend. And He would help them be soooo happy, no matter what!

You are invited to become a
Best Friends Member!

In becoming a member you'll receive a club membership card with your name on the front and a list of the Best Friends and their favorite Bible verses on the back along with a space for your favorite Scripture. You'll also receive a colorful, 2-inch, specially-made I'M A BEST FRIEND button and a write-up about the author, Hilda Stahl, with her autograph. As a bonus you'll get an occasional newsletter about the upcoming BEST FRIENDS books.

All you need to do is mail your NAME, ADDRESS (printed neatly, please), AGE and $3.00 (U. S. currency only) for postage and handling to:

BEST FRIENDS
P.O. Box 96
Freeport, MI 49325

WELCOME TO THE CLUB!

(Authorized by the author, Hilda Stahl)